Tales From The Disenchanted And Wisdom From The *Haiku*

Diana Leavengood Blanco

TABLE OF CONTENTS

PART II
WISDOM FROM THE HAIKU

This book is dedicated to my dear sister, Polly, and
to all those souls whose stories fill its pages....

INTRODUCTION

The Cynic…

Is he but a Disenchanted Romantic?

The Cynic…

Once he DID believe,

But…now…is Disenchanted.

The Cynic…

Tries, still TO believe,

But e'er is Disenchanted.

The Cynic…

WANTS so TO believe,

And NOT be Disenchanted.

But WHAT, in Life,

Can bring him peace,

Now that he's Disenchanted…?

1

Of Philosophies and Musings, and Thoughts on Thoughts and Life

My poems are ofttimes born from some great sadness.
They usually speak of things that have been lost.
They try to catch the soul and trap the memory—
To tell the story...*true*...and—what—the cost.
I rhyme because it helps me to remember.
I rhyme so I must measure every word.
I rhyme to help those lost things live forever,
In rhyming, lilting, steeped-in-meaning verse.
Words can prevail past Flesh, or Thoughts or Empires.
And words can make souls live beyond the grave.
So Man will *ever* KNOW the wonder OF them—
The courage that they showed...the joy they gave.

Rainbows

There's nothing to a rainbow.
So don't go chasing one.
You'll end up with just what you had,
Or…less…when you are done.
You'll be a little older—
A little more worn out—
Perhaps, a little wiser—
Perhaps, just more in doubt.

Keep your nose…there…to the grindstone,
Trudging staunchly on and on.
If you're LUCKY, you'll have made enough…
To be buried when you're gone.

The *Earth's* days are numbered....
We've made sure of *THAT.*
We've stripped Her and scarred Her—
Laid Her on Her back.
She once was our Mother.
Now She's just our Tart.
We've raped and defiled Her.
We've ripped out Her heart.
And, though She's been *silent,*
As we've laid her low.
Someday, She will CALL out—
On THAT day, we'll know
That it is MANKIND
Who will die in the end.
He'll take most life with him—
Be it foe or friend.
The Earth will keep spinning,
She'll dust off Her knees.
Just roaches will flourish
Without many trees.

There are no passions here
Or hereabout.
The long and weary years
Have burned them out.
Instead of raging fires—
Weak, sputtering flames
Expire within,
And hardly have a name.
I cannot still believe in
Anything,
Except that *Change*
Is all that Life will bring.
I speak of love,
But I do not believe.
Man clings to visions
Fashioned to deceive.
My passions—faded, now,
To hopes and dreams
That—tangled in the lies,
Some truth still rings.
The reason Life breeds Life
I cannot see....
Yet Life begets itself
Through history.
I wish for things
We sing of in our songs—
For Beauty that endures,
And Life that's long.
But Life and Beauty
Fade so fast away.
The Darkness always comes,
And, then, holds sway.

The Darkness reigns,
Whether it be Night or Day.
In Darkness, passions drown,
Or lose their way.

Death

Death—so sad, so final—
Yet, sadder…still…
The journey unto Death.
For we are born,
Then we begin to die.
Yet, we must watch so many
Things die FIRST….
Those whom we love,
Our youth,
Our health,
Our beauty and
Our minds
Disintegrate and fade away,
E'er we are allowed to close our eyes
That one last time….
Unless Death takes us
In the bloom of youth…
The sad alternative.

In my attempt to shirk *responsibility*
I come home from *work*, collapse,
And watch "A & E".
I learned about many things…
Then, I forgot,
'Cause Alzheimer's has me cubbyholed
In its slot.
Biographies, court cases, Investigative Reports
Reveal grand heroes…and fiends of every sort.
It's WONDERFUL to know the great and good.
It OVERWHELMS to see the fiends and ghouls.
I've never understood why our society
Spends millions trying to set the villains free
With loopholes, blinded justice—precedent—
In trials where Truth is *inadmissible* evidence.
We spend so *many* millions trying them,
While their victim's bodies are eaten
By the worms.
And…if we find them guilty…
Heaven knows!
In prison, we'll buy their drugs,
T.V.s, and clothes.…

Who said that only Mankind is divine?
Who said that Man is made in the image of God?
And, if that's TRUE, then what does that make God—
A model—vast—of iniquity and sin?
Had I a choice, if…I'd…been making things,
I'd have chosen a different species to mirror me—
Perhaps the penguin, porpoise or the wolf—
A truer soul that seldom kills its own.
But…here we are on *earth*, tooting our horn,
And telling one another we're divine.
It quiets the fear that…maybe…we're not much—
A single blink in the vast expanse of Time.…

Please…let yourself be caught up, day to day,
In the business of surviving the best way.
For, if you are left with too much time to THINK,
You may end up *wiped* out by drugs or drink…
In an effort to forget the *meaninglessness,*
Or to find a *meaning* that can pass the test.
And…if you can't forget, and you can't *find,*
There's always trusty Death to "calm" your mind….

Chain Of Foods...

The Story Of A Tiny Chihuahua,
Her Master, A Boa, And Despair

This story, strange and sad—now full of hate—
Should not have happened, but for twists of Fate.
The summer sun was burning up the land.
Seeking relief, the boa escaped the man.
She travelled helter-skelter down the pike,
Until she found a spot she thought she liked.
Then, silently, she coiled upon a porch,
And there she stayed, avoiding summer's scorch.
When out from doggie door came a tiny pup.
The snake, o'erwhelmed with hunger, scooped her up.
The tiny dog let out a frightened yelp—
So full of pain and fear—begging for help.
Her master, old and feeble, dazed—confused,
Could not decide in time just what to do.
And so, the precious moments slipped away
Wherein she could have saved a life that day.
She never thought to grasp a spade or knife,
And cut the snake and save her puppy's life.
Instead of stopping Fate, there, in Her tracks,
She chose to just record Fate's gruesome acts.
The camera clicked away as her puppy died.
Tears cannot save, though countless tears be cried.
Before you judge. . . 'twas God who put us here
And bade that life eat life, however dear.
And so it is that Man eats furry things—
Cooks them in tantalizing gourmet dreams
And so it is, the snake, without a guise,
Seeks out and eats her prey...for God is wise.
And so it is I ask of you these things:
Forgive the snake for all the pain she brings.

Forgive the man, who never did mean harm.
Forgive the master, frozen with alarm.
As God looked down upon us, none could save
This tiny puppy from her frightful grave.

The Legend of Dracula
Awes and *confounds* the mind—
That a once mortal man could have the power
To rise above both Death…and…Finite Time….
He was just a man who had revered his God,
His Church, his country, and all those he *held dear*.
He was just a man who left his home to fight
The *enemies* that his religion feared.
It was his prowess—not the Hand of God—
That slaughtered them and brought them to their knees,
For the Hand of God was busy weaving *webs*—
In which to *trap* his "faithful" and deceive.
His wife—devoted—was told that he had died,
She cast herself from castle turret—tall,
And drowned in freezing castle moat, below.
He learned his *love* was forever lost to Earth.
He'd have to find her in Eternity.
But his Church told him her soul was ever *damned,*
And that what he *believed* could never be.
His rage welled up and overflowed!
It decimated all!
And, as it rose, it drove his soul
To depths of darkest pall.
And, so it was, that he would never die.
He'd live on living blood forever on.
He'd ever watch the young grow old and die,
And lose all those ever he chose to love.
In *dark*, he drained his victims of their blood,
Or turned them into fiends, likened to him.
He searched the Ages for his beloved wife—
For *centuries* flew the *night*-skies on *batwings.*
But just what WAS he--?
A shadow, *drear*—a creature of the night—

By Love and Valor—damned to Hell,
And banished from the light.
Things *lived*…then *died*.
He watched it all
Throughout the centuries.…
For that's the price he had to pay
For Immortality.

The Beginning, Then, The End

Our attributes when Life begins
Are so like when it ends.
The journey…ofttimes…is long and hard
Between diapers and "Depends".
Though words that describe us sound the same,
The pictures painted, thereby,
Are as *different* as the night is from the day,
As *different* as the truth is from the lies.
Forsooth…a baby has wrinkles and folds,
And…in truth…it can't form words.
The smile it smiles has nary a tooth,
And it knows not what it has just heard.
A baby's helpless—doesn't know its name,
Or what it's looking at.
A baby's life depends on others—
You can depend on that!
A baby cannot sit or stand.
It cannot walk alone.
A baby coos, a baby drools,
And its muscles have no tone.
A baby poops upon itself—
It pees on itself, too.
A baby cannot feed itself—
It can't put on its shoes.
An *old* soul, on the verge of death,
Is *proof* that Life's Great Curse
Is that Man returns to the way he was
When he first arrived on Earth.
But…*now*…no one *admires* these traits,
And no one *oohs* and *aahs!*
They're way too busy *changing* him,
And scarce have time to pause.

But was there something in between?
He cannot say, for sure.
Perhaps Life's one of God's best jokes.
Thank God…now…it's a BLUR!

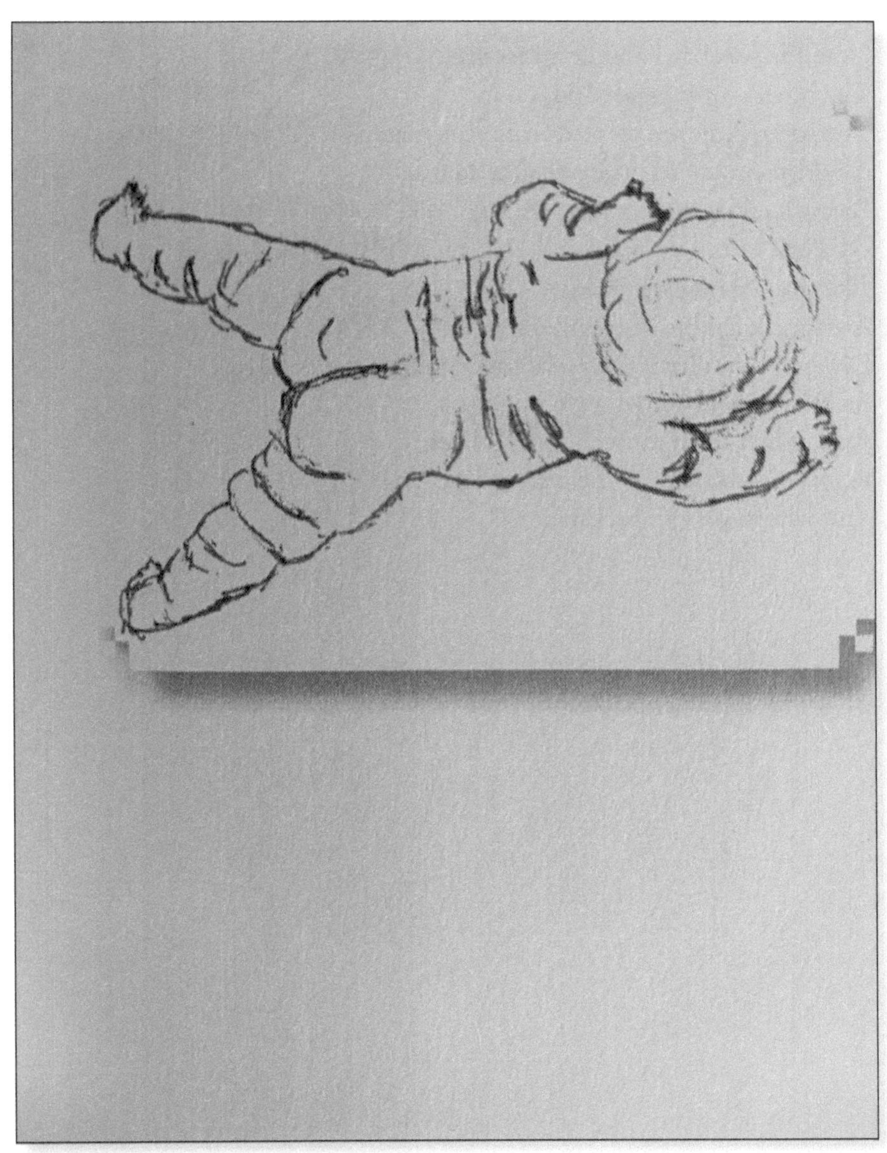

I came from sturdy stock of Nordic hue.
One side was hard and domineering,
The other…quiet and kind.
The seven children created from this match—
All different…. Yet, threads, like Hansel's
Breadcrumbs, make a path through the "Forests
Of Time" to this day.
The strands of generations
Are spun together in a million
Different ways and *different* proportions,
As DNA spells out who we might be,
And…then, each moment of our lives
Points out the way to the next,
And whom we will become.

The MAGIC's *there*—just buried deep
'Neath promises I have to keep,
Beneath the bills I have to pay,
Beneath the worries of the day,
Beneath the things that go awry,
Beneath the failures—though I try,
Beneath the weight that's *piled* on,
Beneath a world so full of *wrong,*
Beneath a chilling loss of faith,
Beneath the thought that Life's a *waste,*
Beneath *responsibilities,*
And grumpy folks I try to please.
I'll *look* for it...when I have time.
It's something I should like to find.

Most times, just where I am, I *want* to be.
I guess that's 'cause I feel "at home" with me.
A canopy of stars, a verdant wood,
A modest home, a mansion—all are good.
More than the *place*, this thing called "home" depends
On how you like yourself and love your friends.
If you are happy with *yourself,* you see,
Then home's whatever place you choose to be.
And should it happen you can't swim the tides,
The blood that courses in your veins provides
A fam-i-ly who offers its strong arms,
A fam-i-ly who can protect from harm.
And, so, the riddle's solved,
And home can be…where'er you are…
Or with your family.

CHAPTER

2

That's Amore

The Secret Of Lasting Love

Two Words—Not *One*

A secret, oh so deep and dark,
To thee, alone, I will impart.
This secret, known to precious few,
Is told, not in *one* word, but *two*.
It has the power to keep love strong
In this old world that's gone all wrong.
One instant more—you'll know the truth,
With no more beating 'round the "bush".
The secret to love's passion be—
To put it straight—IN…*frequently*!

Is He Perfect?

You *seem* to know the words
Before I *say* them,
And games that people play
Before they *play* them.
You know just what I think
Without me *talking*.
And people full of bull
Just send you *walking*.
You make me laugh
In spite of Life's *afflictions*.
You *can't* be true—
I think you must be *fiction!*
Yet…there you are,
Handsome and strong *above* me,
With a soft kiss…sometimes…
To say you *love* me.

Caught Unawares….

I Want To Know Where Love Is

I looked for you
In all the usual places.
But all I found were
Uninspiring faces.
Then—suddenly—a strong hand
Touched my shoulder.
As I looked back to see,
The touch grew bolder.
Your hands began to move—
The fire flying.
The silken web you wove
Left passion sighing.
The Ecstasy I sought
Snuck up behind me.
If ever I get lost,
Make sure you find me.

Just When...

A Middle-aged Love Poem

Just when...it seemed
That all desire had left me.
Just when...stories of Love...I could not grasp.
Just when...true "love knots"
Seemed a dime a dozen.
With ropes that broke,
And ties that did not last.
Just when...Love's pain and suffering
Seemed so foolish,
As did Love's monuments,
Like Taj Mahal.
Just when the empires lost for Cleopatra
Seemed lost...in vain...
For nothing much at all.
And how could Troy be lost for
Theft of Helen,
When there were other beauties
All around?
How could a life be given for just ONE lover,
When lovers by the thousands
Did abound?
Passion had truly died
'Til your hands *touched* me,
And I forgot, in that moment, who I was.
And I forgot I was an *unbeliever*—
A weary soul who had no use for Love.
Your lips seemed just to fit when, first, you kissed me.
They took my breath away,
Then gave it back.
I've never tasted lips
Quite so *delicious*.
And, though I closed my eyes,

Nothing was black.
Your lips moved down my body
Just like cat paws—
So soft and light
While playing with their prey.
But then they struck and held,
And teased, with *claws* out.
The pain—ecstatic—
Took my breath away.
Our time for "young love"—
NOW, is long past over.
No more to think "this is the only one".
And though, with age, our beauty
Fast has faded— Love—
dim the lights— We still
can have some fun!
And do not fear that…I…think
Love will hold us…
One to another for all eternity.
Love binds what it will bind…
And not *forever*….
The Taj Mahal's for others
Not for me.

When, of a sudden, there stood a man who moved me.
Who made me dream and yearn, and think of love.
He came when all my passion had gone *elsewhere*,
And my *desire* for flesh had turned to dust.
But…whoops…he came and went just like a flash flood—
Just like a lightning bug—there—in the night.
He left me with a passion newly wakened.
He lit a fire I had no way to fight.
'Twould have been best to live with senses deadened.
And never again face unrequited love.
But he has made the fire spring from the ashes.
No other hands can do what his touch does.
Now, I must turn to Father Time to save me.
My lover cares not if I live or die.
The hands of Father Time can heal or cripple—
I must trust in them to HEAL, as years go by.

3

Of Mommies, My Children, and Valentines

A Mommy's good for, oh, so many things.
She helps with homework,
Cooks, chauffeurs and cleans.
She pulls out splinters,
Dries sad, teary eyes.
She gives warm comfort,
Praises all the *tries*.
Why does a Mommy
Do these many things?
It *cannot* be for the small *thanks* it brings.
There's just one reason
She bears all this strife.
A Mommy loves her children…
More than Life.…

My daughter called—spoke with a different tone.
Sometimes my children make me feel alone.
But not *today* —she said she loved me true,
And, without me, would not know what to do.
My slender son, with clumping feet like wood,
Stumps through the house...and Life...
Tries to be good...*sometimes*...
When that thought's on his mind...,
But, mostly, clumping—shoelaces dragging behind.
I am so glad *that* they are babes no more.
Caring for *little* ones is such a chore.
I loved it when I did it...now, it's done.
I'm far too old to think of it as fun.
Stuffed animals are cute but gather dust.
And toys can break, wear out or turn to rust...
As *people* can..., so we must try *each day*...
To *do* and *say* the things we *mean* to do and say.

Where's the Ranch?

A Pack Rat's Dilemma

There was "Mom" ...in her nightgown
In the dead of the night.
She had crept to the dumpster—
Thought she was out of sight.
Sifting *through* her bruised treasures—
Much to her great delight—
She had *found* her ranch dressings
In little *packets*, closed tight.
But, alas, in the doorway
With her hands on her hips,
Cold, hard steel in her eyes,
And no smile on her lips,
Stood her *beloved* teenaged daughter,
So "Mom" let out a cry—
For not a *sliver* of kindness
Could she find in those eyes.
"Mother, what are you doing,
Skulking out on the street?"
"Daughter, what are you doing,
Judging, tapping your feet?"
"I've just found my ranch dressings"
Was Mom's courageous reply.
"I'll toss them up in a salad, and I'll give them a try."
"Mother, think what you *will*. Mother, do what you *may*.
If I find any *more*,
I'll, again, throw them away!"

The woodsy smell of pine calls from the past
That *moment* when we rolled car windows down,
As we reached the cool freshness of the Smokey Mountains
From flat, hot, salty Florida in the summers of my youth.....
The sight of my children sleeping—so silent--
Causes a feeling of intense tenderness to
Sweep over me, erasing any anger, or disappointment,
Or cranky criticism, or doubt of Life's worth.
The taste of many things calls up voracious
Appetites that will not be satisfied.
The sound of thundering hooves
And the "call of the race" bring tears...
And dreams of raising a "Champion",
Who will win *against all odds*,
Foretelling what is to be written at my death
About my life. Is it to be,
"She was a dreamer of little substance...
For none of her dreams *ever* came true"?
Or is it to be,
"She was a horsewoman of great wisdom
And renown, for she gave unto this world...
A Champion...?

I once had lots of time to spend with you.
I followed you around—watched over you.
I read to you, just as the experts said.
I sang you *lullabies*—tucked you in bed.
And then, the things all *changed*—I had no time.
With Daddy gone…our lives were on the line.
The bills rolled in, just like the rolling sea—
One, then another, came crashing over me….
I thought I'd *lost* you in the early years.
The crazy things you did confirmed my fears.
But, *somehow*, someway…those simple lullabies
Had nurtured hearts of gold—souls that were wise.
You had the basic *good* to lean upon
When temptations of the world strung you along.
And…so it is…that you've come *back* to me—
The children that I'd always hoped you'd be.

Stuart and Ashley

I'll always wonder if I cursed or blessed you,
When, from my womb, you came into this world.
But always know that I'm so thankful…for you—
My gentle son and rugged little girl.

The Eternal Pact…Did You Know?

I know I've told you…more than once…"I love you".
I know I've told you what you mean to me.
But did you know I'd give my last breath FOR you?
Mothers have done that through eternity.

The Question

To my *teenagers*…
What can I say?
And who would listen,
Anyway?

Oh, I have loved in this brief life—
Loved many and *loved* well.
I weep for some, now lost to me.
They fell beneath Death's spell.
I hold my loves deep in my heart.
I see them in my mind—
So grateful for the "gift" of them—
A gift etched out in Time.
My soul bends 'round,
My mind's eye *strains* to see…
The loves who fly in netherworlds,
Or still walk the earth with me.
And on this day when Love's power *reigns*,
And the Queen of Hearts is King,
I hope they know I love them all
Far more than it may seem.

With sadness all around me,
My heroes mostly gone,
The life I've lived—fast fading,
My time on earth—not long,
There are *still* bright rays of sunshine.
I see them shining through,
In the eyes of my two children,
Dear friends, and family, too.

4

Of Family and Friends

Geneva

A Poem For Our Beloved Ginny

She was our *maid*…in the Old South,
Where black and white were kept *apart*.
We, being kids, had questions—few,
Accepted what was done as *"true"*.
Our Ginny raised us seven kids.
'Twas *she* who knew our ins and outs.
'Twas *she* who fed us…*healed* us, too.
'Twas she who knew just what to do.
More *nurturing* than our *real* mom was—
A wiry worker who never tired.
She always had two open arms,
And words of *comfort* when we cried….
I will never forget the day, at three years old,
When my brother John and I accidentally
Set our neighbor's woods on fire,
And had to watch their trees just burn away.
At tiny table, on tiny chairs, with bologna sandwiches
On our plates, we asked our Ginny all about fires.
She answered *kindly*—never got irate….
My mom was always jealous of the love
Her seven children had for their Ginny.
And, so, she finally let her go.
We *cried* for her, but could not save….
She *blessed* some *other* families…
Taught *other* children to be kind.
Then sickness came to her…and *pain*.
I went to see her one last time.
Not a complaint came from her lips
About *present* pain or pain of Life.
She'd always accepted Life as it came to her,
And *blessed* the world and *us* by who she was.

Edna ("Ted") And Ruie

Grandma Ted and Grandpa Ruie—
That's who they were to me.
But I was just a little girl….and
That's all that I could see.
Now that I've grown and seen the world—
Yes…seen far too *many* things,
I know that they were *special* souls
That are few and far between.
Born way back when the Century turned,
And *honor* still had breath.
They knew of things—*forgotten*, now,
And that love brought *happiness*.
When he *first* saw his Edna Belle
He *could* not catch his breath,
For *she* was the *prettiest* thing he'd seen…
North, South, East or West.
They settled in the Florida sun,
And bought a little farm.
They had two sons—one was my dad—
Raised in strong but gentle arms.
Gramps built a business, repairing shoes.
It was a simple life they lived.
HIS hands of leather—*hers* soft and kind—
That never refused to give.
One time he gave some land away
To a neighbor 'cross the way.
Now…such a thing would never be.
But it was "back in the day" ….
Ruie's mother had been a *wild* thing.
She left her little boy.
She played her hand out in the world.
So, he became his grandfolks' joy.
When she came back …he took her in—

No *lists* of rights or wrongs.
He *cared* for her until she died…
In diapers, but not *alone*….
We *loved* to visit their warm home—
Hear stories of the past,
And all the old-time thoughts and ways
That haven't seemed to last. What—
you must ask—set them apart? Their
lives seemed plain, you see.
But *goodness* lived *wherever* they *were*—
Broad as the boundless sea.
They never said a word…*unkind*…
Even when it was *deserved*.
Their hearts—so gentle, souls—so kind.
Honor bound by just their word….
When Grandma fell, and couldn't walk,
He carried her for years
From bed to bath, and back again,
With no complaint or tears.
And when she left for *netherworlds*,
He puttered here and there.
A smile was always on his lips—
His mind still kept her there.
And then…his hip was broken, too.
In *bed* he *would* not stay.
He told the nurse he would not eat,
And quietly passed away.
Their two fine sons, and we *grandkids*
Know what *great jewels* we had—
Our loving, gentle grandmama,
And our true and strong granddad….

Flying Richie Home

A Poem For My Beloved Father,
C. Richard Leavengood

Born of two hearts o'erfilled with love,
And four hardworking hands—
My father made his way through life,
A kind and quiet man.
His high school days were happy days.
He worked in this father's shop.
He served his country when it called.
And then, he studied law.
All that he had was what he'd made
From his own industry.
Astride a horse, he looked like Roy,
Autry, or Cassidy.
His quiet good looks and honest charm
Soon won my mother's heart.
She came from wealth, just newly earned,
Dwelt in the "upper crust".
Her father helped them build a house
That overlooked the bay.
A house—more "modern" than practical,
Where…soon…seven children played.
And I was one of the lucky ones
Dad bounced upon his knee,
As he waded through the courts, and Life,
And loved his family.
And he became the first Republican
To become a Florida circuit judge
Since that dreadful, tragic Civil War…
That brought *tears*, killed *flesh*, spilled *blood*….
And all we children love our dad,
Wherever we might go—
He had changed our diapers, held our hands--

So steady—when we were low.
My love for horses came from him,
Along with other gifts.
So, I embraced horseracing's world—
Accepted all its risks.
I named my horses after him
In hopes that Luck would smile.
But Luck is fickle. Luck is coy—
Left me with toil and trial.
When cancer came, he fought so long,
He faded all away.
So thin, so weak, but…still…so dear---
So dear 'til that last day.
They called my sister that sad day
When he drew his last breath.
I think he needed her great heart
To fend off fears of death.
He heard her voice behind closed eyes.
He had waited for her to come.
His hand in hers—some shallow breaths—
And…then, the race was run.…

Stuart, Diana, Ashley and Polly

My Polly Anna

A Poem For My Sister—So Beloved

The burdens of the world
Lay…heavy…on her.
She'd always help,
And never turn away.
And not by someone's merit
Would she judge him—
Just helped and loved
Forever and a day.
And I am honored
I can call her 'sister'.
And I am blessed
More than a thousandfold.
For, rare, upon this earth
A soul doth wander…
Whose goodness far outshines
The brightest gold.

But The Fellas Call Him "Bill"

He makes the saying 'last but not least'
The *truest* of *all* tales.
My youngest brother captains a ship
With talent at its sails.
He was a lark, a comic—clown—
When just a little boy.
One *talent* is…he can change "plain"
To fun, laughter, and joy.
He has a flare for writing things
That subtly mess with Life.
He has a knack for showing things
In dark but *too true* light.
Yet on the edge of all his work
A *chuckle* lurks—a *grin*.
He writes, he acts, he teaches 'Life'.
His students worship him.
He sends them out into the world
With talents finely honed.
Their writing…acting bring them fame,
But it's not theirs, alone.
And he, himself, courts worldwide fame.
It beckons, teases—spins.
The doors creak open, then seem to close…
Just as he's stepping in.
Already famous in our world
For all he has become—
Best dad, best teacher, beat writer, best friend….
He signed it all "With Love".

Swamps And Minds Of Men

Donald—
my friend—eccentric—by the by. Folks
blame it all on 'Nam, but that's a lie.
In woods, he lives with dogs—nor any man,
Digs bullets and the Past whene'er he can.
He's so soft-spoken—his accent—so *gentile.*
Beneath it, *anger* lurks—and iron will.
He knows the battles, generals, and the scores.
He knows the swamps where deadly bullets hide—
The campgrounds, marches—*who…how many* died.
He thinks we're reincarnate—he and I.
That Barlow lives again, and loves his bride.
His storytelling powers—beyond compare.
Alas…his mind is trapped in its own lair.
He calls from time to time to say "hello".
We talk just as we did so long ago.
I chide him about his *eccentricity.*
It's all in fun—he goes *along* with me.
He tells me this and that—I tell him, too.
We wish each other well when we are through.
There really is a genius living there….
It's just…he's lost his mind… most of his hair.

Jennifer

The radiant bloom of youth
Lay…softly…upon you,
Shone from your face,
And clung to every pore.
It caught the eye
Of Something great
And powerful….
He carried you in His arms
To Heaven's door.
So swept away…,
I guess He was not *thinking*
Of those who loved you
That were left behind.
So, they were left to ponder
Whys and wherefores,
To see if hidden answers
They could find.
Four children—fair of face,
With hair that's golden,
A husband who loved true,
And never strayed,
A mom and dad who thought
The sun set on you…
Were forced to lay your body
In the grave.
Yet, in their souls,
Your radiant beauty's shining.
And, in their hearts, your memory
Still lives on.
Your bloom of Youth and Love,
That never faded,
Will whisper comfort to them
Their lives long.

With skin as fine as porcelain,
Wide eyes of azure blue,
Rapunzel hair that lived and shined,
Full lips…kissed by the dew.
And *Youth* clung to her with His might,
For she was, oh, so fair.
He could not turn His eyes away
From this beauty, beyond compare.
But Father Time, and Fortune…cruel
Are not so easily *swayed*.
They conquer Beauty…Wonder…Grace,
Then lay them in the grave.
They ravage creatures—*exquisite*,
Nor do They show remorse.
They banish *Youth* to forests of gloom
Without shield or sword or horse.
And, with our Champion lost in the dark,
Beauty is *sacrificed*—
Damned to the mazes of Father Time,
And *caught* in Fortune's vice.
And now, her eyes are not so blue,
Her skin is not so fine.
Her lips have thinned, so has her hair,
In Nature's cruel design.
The young grow old so there'll be room
For new Life to be born.
The young must watch all that they were
Fade to a thing…forlorn.
The end is not a pretty sight—
Our Destiny…unblessed…
To walk in Beauty…decay with Age…
Before we dance with Death….

Forever Friends

A Poem For My College Roommate—Judith Music

Forever friends—if "forever" really is.
And…if it's not…,
Then, as long as it can be….
Your depth and wit are dazzling.
I love your impish charm!
We walked the quads of dear old Duke.
We walked them, arm in arm.
I followed you about the South—
Farmville and Charlottesville.
While you worked to get your Masters' degree,
I served up restaurant swill.
'Twas then our gentle Johnny came.
He won your heart and hand.
Though you both said that I could stay,
I set out 'cross the land.
The miles and different journeys parted us,
But the wonder of you stayed.
We both had children—light of our lives.
We both had our parts to play.
You dabbled in witchcraft—the kind that's good.
You studied acupuncture, too.
It gave you the knowledge to treat Man's ills,
And lessen his pain, too.
From Boston to the green hills of Vermont,
You and Johnny made your way.
There, may your spirit ever soar, as your red hair fades away.

Like chiming bells, such virtual *pearls*
Of *wisdom* she casts out.
If she'd learn to *follow* her own advice,
It would keep the "faux pas" out.
Her proverbs teach me much of Life,
And, most times, make me laugh.
Her thoughts on Life are such a kick—
Can *save* a sorry ass.
A stubborn streak, when she was young
Oft caused much *harm* and *angst*....
She drove her car on airy fumes...
Refused to fill the tank.
And, so, on side streets...freeways, too,
In sunshine, dark and rain,
Her car would come to a dead stop.
It...one time...faced a *train!*
She was quite full of *devilment*
When just a little girl.
Her younger brother *looked* to her,
Thought she was all the world.
She'd crawl upon her hands and knees,
When her daddy fell asleep,
Just to purloin his *pocket change*...
Her "style of life" to keep.
Then, a *woman—charming, devious*—
Wooed *her* poor *dad* away.
She caught him in her selfish web,
And...there...she made him stay.
So, Life became a tougher deal.
Her mom had tougher chores—
To make her way through life, alone,
And raise a *little* girl and boy.
One of the *wisest* things Di said—

One of the *funniest,* too…
Is that a *"peehole"* can't *hold* a man.
Boy, that's a statement—true!
I'll cherish Di for *all my life.*
She's such a special friend.
Together we will laugh and cry,
And struggle 'til the end.

Dick Eagle And Sally

For Two Of My Heroes

A girl named Luanne…is my best friend.
She is a gift to me.
The *gift* is her unswerving love,
And that of her family.
Her mom and dad are sent from heaven.
Each has a special power.
Sally—the quiet glue of Life.
Richard—the unfazeable tower.
Her dad is truly loved by all.
He has such gentle ways.
And, yet there's strength and steady calm
That brings comfort to our days.
Her mother always stands behind,
And never vies for fame.
Her shoulders carry heavy loads,
Yet seldom does she complain.
Our dads were lawyers, back when…*lawyers*
Stood for upright things….
Back when your word was *good enough…*
Back when truth *soared* on wings.
But now, those simpler times are gone—
Too many people here.
Too many billion hands reach out,
And too few people care.
There is no way to mend the rifts
In our society.
Our heroes, one by one, pass on.
It seems so sad to me.
One of my greatest heroes, yet,
Now faces Father Time.
His family forms a human shield
As he steps up to the line.

There is no finer man alive—
Nor will there ever be.
I hope he knows how much he's loved
By *everyone*...and me....

Luanne and Diana

My Bestest Friend

A Poem For Luanne Eagle Ferguson

Sometimes…angels…are found on earth.
I know that it can be…
Because my "bestest" friend is one,
With sparkle on her wings.
Her parents, uncles, and her aunts
Are of such quality…that…
No words in all the land can tell—
Or in the seven seas.
From loving home, from brightest minds
Came wondrous sisters…three—
Luanne, the thinker,
Artistic Elsie, and little sister Katie.
Each had such special gifts
They got from mystic genes and love.
Their parents' wisdom taught them, well,
What "goodness" is made of.
Luanne and I shared high school years,
Then hitched across the world.
Our lives were ofttimes mirrors—reflections cast—
Since we were but mere girls.
She practices law—wills and estates.
Her mom and dad did, too.
She helps her clients through hard times.
I've seen what she can do.
She has two children—so do I—
All…wonders of the world.
Hers are the champions of all that's good.
In mine, beat tender hearts.
She is so capable in law and life,
With a heart that gives and gives—
A sense of humor to match it all,
But a memory we must forgive.

The stories of the things she's lost
Can make us laugh to tears—
Her car keys, her purse, her passport, her mind
Have escaped her through the years....
Months can go by, yet, when we speak,
It seems like yesterday,
As we share the stories of our lives—
Joys and sorrows, day to day.
And I will always think of her
As a great gift to me.
Surely, magic passed from her mom and dad
To these loving sisters—three.

Felix and Diana

I Have A Friend

My Birthday With Felix Starr Law

I have a friend
Who took me to a place
That overlooked *Nature*...
In all her power and grace.
As waves rolled up,
Then crashed upon the shore,
We tipped our glasses—
A toast to Life, and to a Hope there's something more.
It was my birthday—
Older than I ever wished to be.
And he had come to *celebrate* with me.
Through all our years
His words were kind and wise.
This time I listened...scarce with breath...
As he looked into my eyes.
And, as he spoke, my soul filled up with tears.
The words he *spoke* will not
Fade through the years.
"A birthday is a special day—that's clear.
But it's most *special* to the child,
And the one who brought him here—
To the mother who carried him *nine months*
In her womb—
To the mother, whose body nurtured him
As he grew.
But, though a birthday's *really* between these two,
There are a few exception...,
And one of them is you.
You see, I am so *thankful* you were born,
And that I've come to call you 'friend'
In this old world—forlorn—
That your birthday has become
The most *special* day to me.
It *has been*...*is*...and it will *ever* be...."

CHAPTER

5

Of Princesses, and Legends, and Stars Who Have Walked Among Us

---

My Hero

A Poem For Ennis Cosby

"He was my hero…"
Oh, such powerful words!
The father spoke them—meant them to be heard.
He'd watched his son's *birth*—miracle of life.
Those mystic genes, from husband and from wife,
Mixed in an instant to create a *man*—
And only one…like him…in all the land.
He grew in beauty in body and in soul.
He conquered demons—laid Fate's curses low.
But Fate grew jealous of his strength and charms.
So, Fate reached out and clasped him in Her arms.
As dark of night set in, She dropped him there…
On lonely road, *smack* in harm's way,
And in the dragon's lair.
And who should be there…waiting…but dark Death.
He takes the worst of us—He takes the best.
But, on this night, He claimed His greatest prize—
Our only son—a hero…in…my…eyes.

Linda, My Love, My Champion, My Life….
Linda, My Love, My Champion…My Wife

A Poem For Linda McCartney
September 24, 1941-April 17, 1998

She did love Life, but…more…all living things.
Her strength drew, like a magnet, "starlit" beings.
And one such star tripped on his love and fell.
Just to be near her, he would ride through Hell.
For nigh on thirty years, they held on tight--
Embraced those things they loved with all their might.
They loved their children, and Earth's "children", too.
And for these children, did all they could do.
Their gentle natures guided them to save
The creatures *Man's reign* destines for the grave.
For all these creatures—*helpless* against Man—
They fought as champions, steady in their stand.
And nothing came between them—these two souls—
Not hell, high water, or the winding road.
And when the scourge of cancer laid her low,
Still…she fought on 'til it was time to go.
She left this world holding her true love's hand.
Her spirit rides, unfettered, 'cross the land.

**Diana, Princess Of Wales
The Fairy Must Have Lied**

July 1, 1961-August 31, 1997

Born on that isle set in a silver sea
To *family* of noble *dignity.*
A *prince* there came…on polo pony…not on horse,
Leaned down and swept her up and set their course.
Their wedding—the most *wondrous* one in years—
Was bought with English toil and English tears.
Two princes born…she *bloomed* in motherhood—
Her smile—so sweet, it *seemed* her life was good.
In life, what seems to be, so seldom is….
Deep sorrow dwelt in her eyes—blame—in his.
The love, if ever there, began to fade.
Alas… their marriage not in heaven made.
She called upon her strength, and it was there.
She stood against the Crown and her despair.
She used her vibrant soul to carry *love*
To hapless beings sent here from above.
She won the admiration of the world,
As, on she travelled, heart and soul unfurled.
But, for *herself,* she yearned for peace and love.
She searched through kingdoms…here…and up above.
'Twas on the verge of finding happiness
That her most ardent *suitor* was Dark Death.
And it was He…who carried her away,
And left the world…*forlorn*, in its dismay….

What Child Is This?

A Poem For Michael Jackson
August 29, 1958-June 25, 2009

From Gary, Indiana…to the stars.
His journey—hard—with many twisted turns.
His shields bashed in by belts and cords and iron.
His battered soul…laid out…on Earth to burn.
He recognized the pain that Nature deals.
He took it to his heart, and there it stayed.
It turned him into something *vulnerable*—
A child-like soul who…many fiddlers paid.
His wounded soul nurtured great talent—true.
A talent—*unsurpassed*—that changed the world.
Of dance and song and glitter, he was King.
But Fame oft deadly *Legions* with it brings.
He loved with tender love that had no guile.
The secrets that he kept were of different sorts.
He changed his face to wipe the tears away.
It did not work—just hastened his last day.
His friends—some giants, some just common folk,
Seemed bound to him with steel-like threads of gold.
But even…they…could not keep *hungry* wolves away.
The wolves sought out this lamb—*devoured* their prey.…
The things he treasured most—all left behind.
Those things are not of *gold and silver* made.
His children, mother, sister…truest friends—
Those are the things he loved to his last day.

A Poem For John F. Kennedy, Jr. And All The Kennedys
November 25,1960-July 16, 1999

Life "On The Edge" ...now that's a thought—
A *choice*...in modern times.
In olden times, with war and pestilence,
Life was *always* on the line.
Technology and the wealth of Man
Make ease and extra time,
And have dulled "The Edge",
So, now, some seek those "rushes" near *sublime*.
To *climb* a mountain, infamous,
To *surf* up in the sky,
To *dive* the dark bowels of the sea,
To *drive* past speeds, untried,
To *bounce* at end of bungee cord,
To *fly* the fastest plane—
Some men have need for something *wild,*
Now that survival is tame.
Man *seldom* has a predator,
Lest it be another man.
Man's food is killed in slaughterhouses,
So, easily, comes to hand.
We need not fear the sabretooth.
Our genius fights disease.
Our right hand surfs the internet
To find things, as we please.
And, so, there are a few bold souls
Who can't bear this dull life.
They find their meaning "On The Edge" ...
Their glory in the strife.
And, so it seems, the Kennedy clan,
Secured by wealth and fame,
Has need to seek things—unsecured—

To know those things—untamed.
Secret intrigue, The Mafia,
Fast sport, and faster planes
Have taken lives…just in their prime—
Caused those left here great pain.
This last game was the saddest, yet,
Because it took away…
Two beauties…just there for the ride…
Who did not need to play.

Larger Than Life

A Poem For Wilt Chamberlain
August 21, 1936-October12. 1999

Larger than Life—indeed, he was—
And, so, it seemed to me.
I met him once. I liked his voice…
And his eyes, as he looked at me.
I always thought he was the sort
Of man that I'd admire.
I wish I could have known him well—
Shared the soul that has so inspired.
But in this life of *boundaries*,
Of duties, place, and Time,
We cannot share in all the lives
That strike us as so fine.
I could fill a book—or a thousand days
With the folks I wish I'd known—
To have learned from them—to have taught them, too,
To have shared thoughts like my own.
It seems so sad when the great ones go.
We want them to go on—
To be the heroes for us all…
To lay our garlands on.
My life…inconsequential…next to his.
The things I've done seem small.
If only I could have known the man
Before this last curtain call.

Total Yardage—The Measure Of A Man

A Poem For Walter Payton
July 25, 1954-November 1, 1999

A Legend—yes—
Yet…still…he was a man—
A man so kind and gentle,
Yet…so strong.
He quietly set new records
That still astound.
But conceit and arrogance
Never turned his head around.
He moved with grace in Life,
And on the field.
He played his *cards* well—
Not complaining about the 'deals'.
He never cheated,
Or ever used sleight of hand.
And, soon, there gleamed a Legend—
Where…once…there'd stood just a *man*.
Now, the *man* is gone,
But the Legend still lives on.
May his super-human feats forever be told.
May his goodness ever be measured in miles—not yards.
May we never forget how he faced Death
With all his courage.

Dandy Don

A Poem For Don Meredith
April 10, 1938-December 5, 2010

Ole Dandy Don! What's in a name—
Football, good humor…fun?
Yes, Dandy Don was all of these,
As…through life…he made his run.
He started out at SMU,
And there, became a star.
The Dallas Cowboys wanted him.
He was their *golden* boy.
For ten years more, he threw the ball—
Most times, he threw it…straight
Into his teammates open arms.
The fans thought he was *great*!
He dabbled in a lot of things.
His easy-going ways
Opened up doors, and widened paths
In the "entertainment" moves he made.
Then, he took on the NFL
In quite a different way.
His commentary Monday Night
Just blew the fans away!
He brought the laughter, brought the warmth…
Made Howard and Frank…cringe and smile,
And *"Monday Night"* is not the same…
Without him, this long while.
Frank Gifford was crying when he told
The world that he had lost his friend,
And how he'd loved him all those years…
Until his untimely end.

Elizabeth

A Poem For Elizabeth Edwards
July 3, 1949-December 7, 2010

How brave she was…how beautiful,
How full of what inspires.
She made *firm ground* of shifting sands
That plagued her as a child.
Without a rudder steering straight,
And stormy, frightening seas,
Her childhood days brought little peace,
Security or ease.
She grew in grace…,
She had the "smarts", the drive, the energy.
She had her family and friends,
Hope, and resiliency.
She was to need…all…of these things,
As Life dealt out the cards.
She *cherished* all that she found good.
Stood *strong* when things got hard.
She celebrated doing right.
She tried her best to be…
A beacon for the drowning souls,
Tossed in Life's stormy seas.
And…so…she was. She gave us much—
Of courage…. Taught us well….
A woman, "most remarkable",
As history books will tell….

Of Our Valiant Soldier Boys

Our Georgia Soldier Boy

A Poem For Joe Moore

From the fragrant pines of Georgia
To Iraq's vast, burning sands,
They have made a SOLDIER of me,
With no rifle in my hands.
Instead, I fixed the engines
That helped keep our troops alive.
Instead, I patched the motors
That delivered our supplies.
For a while there was a *curtain*,
And it hid the raw, sad truth.
I had felt secure—protected—
In my mechanics-specialist group.
But, then, we ventured to the field,
Saw once-warm bodies…cold and still.
A new awareness gripped me—
And it was a bitter pill….
I long for home…so far away,
And the life that I left there…
The wonders of computer worlds,
Fast cars…less deadly cares.
I'll shrug off fear as best I can, Stand tall and do my time.
But, when I sleep, the dreams I dream
Are of my Georgia pines.

A Soldier's Story

A Poem For Gerard Wyss

He volunteered...a Specialist...
When World War II began.
When he got hurt, they *discharged* him,
Then *reenlisted* him once again.
He was always mechanically inclined,
And of high intelligence.
But would the army notice this,
And do *something* that made sense?
I guess it made a *little* sense.
He was sent to the Ardennes...
A place they told him was deemed "safe",
On France's borderlands.
No maps, no compass, no radio,
And just a water truck,
Where he filtered water for our troops to drink.
He had ONE gun...for luck.
He and his buddy set the "water point" ...
Confiscated an old mill.
They told the miller their "boss" would pay,
So, he would bode no ill.
Their rations came in boring cans.
They thought it might be fun
To search for big deer in the woods.
After all...each had a gun.
With seven *other* soldiers, in their teens,
They killed a giant stag.
The butcher had made a deal with them,
But there was just one little snag.
They'd been told the *Germans* were "all through",
And the war was almost done.
Turns out *intelligence* was wrong—
The Krauts *weren't* on the run.

Instead, they came…A-MARCHING down
The lane above the mill,
With two machine gun and many men…
The young soldiers…all felt ill.
They gathered 'round the oldest man.
They sought his best advice.
He thought a moment, then uttered the words
That—surely—saved their lives.
"We'll hunker down behind the grain.
We'll make each bullet count.
Don't raise your heads above the bags….
We must take the machine guns out."
The young boys did just what he asked.
They waited in silent fear.
The snow had melted, so the German's white camouflage
Was not the proper gear.
Three shots took out the first machine gun.
And Jerry took the last.
The Germans tried to reengage.
The time for that had passed.
The Americans took them, one by one.
The Germans were mystified.
They never saw an enemy…
Just saw their comrades die.
The last of them began to run
O'er the hill from which they came.
Jerry had saved those seven boys…his partner…
And stamped a name.
This story…true…was seldom told.
The glory never given…
As it was born of an illegal hunting trip
That sent Germans to hell…or heaven.
Gerard went back, and found the mill,
When the strife had long been o'er.
And, though the miller had not been paid,
Still, he opened wide his door.

The people living in the woods
Of the dark and dense Ardennes
Remembered the Americans as "Freedom's Champs",
And still thought of them as friends....

Our Knight in Shining Armor

To the Memory of Ricky Slocum
February 2, 1985-October 24, 2004

Made of the upper air,
Sunshine, and light—
A child *fashioned* from
Every mother's dream—
With eyes of blue, and
A smile so warm and real,
A body…strong…and goodness
You could *feel*.
He was my son's good friend
As little boys. Then, later on,
Life's trials brought him my way.
He needed a safe harbor
From the storms—a room, a roof,
A place where he could stay.
So, I was blessed with knowing
Who he was. The darkness
Gathered…tried to steal his light.
The soul within him was
So strong and true….it battled
Back, and soundly won the fight.
He had a dream to be
A shining knight—protector
Of ideals America holds dear.
'Twas on his quest to stand
Against our foes, that Death
Came 'round and laid
Our hero low.
So, in his prime and in
The throes of Life…e'er giving,
Striving, loving, being loved—

This precious soul, who'd had
It's hills to climb,
Was taken from us—
With *no* good reasons *why*….

Of Things that Should Not Have Been

The Visitor

A Poem For Anthony Michael Martinez

A twist of Fate so cruel to cause alarm.
A child was ripped out of his family's arms
By something vile and evil, that was spawned
Upon this earth to perpetrate great harm.
Just how it is such things can ever be
Cannot be understood by you or me.
And, oh, it seems too much to understand
Such evil lurks and hides in shape of Man.
A vile, demented creature—full of hate—
Ascended out of hell and tempted Fate
To turn the other way, and then he stole
A precious life…battered a precious soul.
A boy whose face shone with such radiant light
Was ripped and torn by deadly evil might.
His body bore a story of such pain,
The horror of it always will remain.
A slender body, found amongst the stones,
Bereft of life and all that it had known.
That never will again feel warmth or love,
Whose soul has flown away on wings of doves.

Lament For A Boy—Lost...

A Poem for Lamoun Thames

The value of a life? A subject, deep....
Nor does the value tell who we can keep.
The value of a child, when parents love,
Cannot be measured here, or up above.
Just such a child was cruelly whisked away
As, to a better life, he made his way.
His momma loved him since he first drew breath.
She taught him everything she thought was best.
She sacrificed, so he could know the way
To be the best he could be every day.
He waited at the stop that fateful night—
So full of hope—his dreams now taking flight.
Then, for some reason we cannot surmise,
A demon came—claimed for himself this prize.
Now, years gone by, a million tears have dried.
In years to come, a million will be cried.
At last, we've found the "thing" that took his life.
We found him guilty—he killed with a knife.
He's guilty, though, of such a heinous thing,
His verdict will not ever Justice bring.
For all his days, he'll ride upon our backs,
With all the comforts, paid for by our tax.
But for the child he killed—no comfort comes—
In darkness...cold, alone...his life undone.

The Futile Vigil

A Poem For Matthew Louis Checci

Two coal-black horses
Galloped *swiftly*
O'er the sand.
With their huge strides,
They covered many miles.
Their masters did not have
To urge them on....
They came upon some tents and motor homes—
A place where people try to "get away".
This time, there would be one who would never return.
THIS death would have no sense, with no lesson learned....
They passed the guard, who slumbered at the gate.
They passed by the aunt, who dutifully did wait.
Disguised in the trappings of a *drifter*, They entered there,
And, with Their power, loosened a great Despair...
That caught—within its grip—a *family*,
And made of all our sense...a *mockery*.
The aunt—a few feet away—
Not more—
Stood silent vigil
Outside the bathroom door.
Insanity is cunning....
Death is vile....
As They swept past,
They turned to hide their smiles.
They slit a throat from ear to ear—
The aunt—too late—though, oh, so near.
A life, so full of promise and light,
Could not be saved by Might or Right.

A young boy died…there…on the floor
In loving arms he'd feel no more….
You cannot e'er too careful be…
When *Death* rides with *Insanity*.
As all our truths are blown away,
The sun sets on another day….

Lay Me Down Gently

A Poem For Nicholas Markowitz

They laid him down in his own grave,
And then they slaughtered him.
At Lizard's Mouth, he met his death—
'Twas for another's sin.
His mouth was taped,
His hands were bound…,
Alas…his mind was free…
To contemplate his coming end,
To know what was to be.
It must have wandered—desperate—
Not knowing how to hide
From Death, Who looked down on him
From once-kind human eyes.
How could it be that childhood friends,
With whom he'd had such fun,
Would now be standing over him…,
With the barrel of a gun?
He was just a child who'd done no wrong,
But became the *sacrifice*
For a brother who had fallen prey
To drugs, avarice, and vice.
And…what of these *creatures*—children, too,
Who caused this death…this strife?
Did they believe the grudge they held
Was worth this young boy's life?
I guess they did…so this child died—
Laid out in his own grave.
No one on earth can find good cause.
No one on earth could save….

The Playground

A Poem For Blaine Talmo, Jr.
And Chris McCulloch

Two boys—so young—
Who thought they might be *men,*
Dabbled in drugs—
Could not gage foe or friend.
Out on the lam,
And testing their new wings…
Making mistakes
This transformation brings.
They thought they knew it all—
Too young for doubt.
But when *Death* began to stalk them,
They called out.
Their cell phone gave a voice
To silent fear.
The friend who listened
Heard the message…clear…
That someone *followed*—
Someone…cloaked in Night.
Through all their veins
There flowed a breathless fright.
Their friend could not save them—
Young lives met their end—
Bludgeoned and bloodied—
No one to defend.
On lonely playground…there…
They lost their lives.
Their blood was shed
'Neath only *Heaven's* eyes.
Now, thoughts of manhood
Never cross their minds,
Nor any other thought

Of any kind.
Their lifeless bodies
Tell what's not to be—
Two babes struck down
By human cruelty.

Where Are The Whys And Wherefores?

A Poem For Laurie Miles And Her Son

He killed her—shot her in cold blood—
Without a second thought.
He wondered—should he spare the child,
Or kill him for the sport?
His friend told him, "Leave him alone".
And, so, a life was spared.
The killer let the child live,
But not because he cared.
A mother—dead—and no good cause.
A son now scarred for life.
'Twas just outside a bible school
That they were sacrificed.
We wonder how this e'er could be,
And, then, we wonder why.
We wonder who deals out the cards,
And why things go awry....
Two weeks went by—the killer hid—
This tale not at its end.
His hate rose up and killed a girl
Who...once...had been his friend.
A human form—without a soul—
Wreaked vengeance on this Earth.
We wonder where he lost his soul...
In his life or before his birth?
Humanity has ever embraced
So many sorts of men....
The blessed...unblessed...the greats...the fiends
Are born time and again.
We do not know which ones will save—
Which ones will slaughter us.
We cannot figure out the "whys",
Although we feel we must.

Immortal...? Maybe Not....

A Poem for Kali Manley

She thought she had the world...
There...in her hands.
Youth gives false power.
Youth fails to understand.
Youth made her think
That she knew all the scores.
It whispered, "You're all that,
All that...and more".
She threw all care and caution
To the wind.
A door swung wide—naïve—
She entered in.
She thought it was the door
To fun and games.
But she was wrong....
It led to death and pain....
The arrogance of Youth
Is, oh, so *bold!*
It will not listen—
Refuses to be told.
Youth thinks that grown-ups
Haven't got a clue.
Youth *blasts* through Life,
Judgement—values—askew.
Youth's uncaged fury,
And its unbridled power
Deplete its ranks—
Its own *firm flesh* devour.
And the survivors...?
Finally...they are grown—
Circle of Life—
Have children of their own.

If Only

A Poem For Ryan Harris And Her Mother

Her arms, that once embraced the world,
Lie motionless at her sides.
She'd only meant to ride her bike,
But on Death's horse did ride.
How can a thing you love so much
So *suddenly* be gone?
What is the reason,
What…the rhyme?
I'll wonder my life long.
A mother's heart now labors
Just to beat,
For, with her child, the meaning
Passed away….
And thoughts pursue her…
As wild dogs stalk their prey.
The thoughts do not *uplift,*
They just devour.
They tease her with what
Might or could have been.
Her eyes—dull red—
Look out…seem not to see.
Her lips—so pale—*move…*
Yet…seem not to speak.
The words they form
Just barely have a sound.
The cadence is *uneven,*
HEAVY…Slow….
"If I…could just…erase
One hour…or change
Her steps in time…."
"If…I…could just erase…
One hour…or change…
Her…steps…in…time."
"If…I could just erase…that hour…."

'Twas The Night Before Christmas

Her eyes—how they sparkled.
Her dimples—how deep.
Her lips—red as roses.
Her smile—full and sweet.
With a long, graceful neck,
And fine skin—oh, so fair,
A sparkly demeanor,
And dark, shining hair.
Oh, she was a beauty—
Both *inside* and *out!*
And, when she went missing,
Everyone looked about…
To try to discover
The place she could be….
Four months later, they found her
By the side of the sea.
Her tragic remains
Washed up—there—on the shore…,
And the tiny remains
Of her unborn little boy,
There was little recognizable
About the corpses they found,
But forensics determined
They were Laci and her child.
Yet…who could have killed
Such a beauty…and why?
'Twas the *fiend* in men's clothing
Who had stood at her side.
'Twas the one who had promised
"Until death…do…us…part",
And, when he kept that promise,
He broke the world's heart.

In An Instant

A Poem For Eve Carson

The planets, stars, the sun, the moon
Must all have smiled that day.
The day when heaven came down to earth,
And "Eve" became her name.
She grew in beauty and strength of will.
Her goodness knew no bounds.
So *bright,* the world lay at her feet.
Her genius shown like a crown.
No arrogance in any fiber,
But *grace* in every move.
All unaware she was a "gift",
And not simply a "girl".
The gift was given, then nurtured, here,
On earth's unholy ground.
The gift was taken, just as it bloomed—
Our senses—to confound.
For what Great Power, what Mighty Hand
Would sculpt a form—sublime,
Then set it in the dragon's lair
With no weapon of any kind?
And how could such a precious being,
Whose love had the power to save,
Be snuffed out by such lowly souls—
Her light flickering—in the grave.

Who can explain it,
When answers can't be found—
The helpless stare, the hopeless shrug,
When Reason finds no ground?
Two girls—their lives beginning—
Futures bright,
A mom, whose life…so far…,
Played out just right….
And then, some mighty evil
Came along.
But we have yet to see its face
Or hear its hideous song….
Cloaked in great mystery,
They disappeared…
Midst beauty—stately, calm—
Nature revered.
They'd had such great fun…,
But…that faded fast,
In final hours of dread,
When hope had passed.
This mighty evil
In the trappings of Mankind
Dealt in such terror
It breaks the spirit,
And confounds the mind.
Imagination tries not to take us there—
To those last hours, overfilled with such despair.
It stops us short—
It turns our eyes away—
The horror and pain…too great on that last day.

Epilogue

The killer was finally found, but only after he
had violently murdered naturalist Joie Ruth Armstrong....

95

The Aggies' Tragedy

A pile of logs—not such a deadly thing—
A celebration that *long tradition* brings.
A center-pole of timber, bolts and steel
Breaks up beneath the strain,
So, twelve are killed.
That simple bonfire, lit so long ago,
Grew monstrous in its size and fiery glow.
Each year…the Aggies tried to beat the last.
They tried to build a bigger pile.
They tried to best the past.
Sometimes, the biggest isn't always best.
And…sometimes…more…can be far worse than less.
To build the biggest fire—what does that mean--?
Just that you've built the biggest fire
Texas has ever seen.
Some people looking on may say, "Who cares?"
Still…others…might be overwhelmed—
Transfixed—with wide-eyed stares.
With cautious wisdom, the pile was whittled down,
In hopes of keeping its builders safe and sound.
Alas—the best-laid plans of mice and men
Sometimes, work out—sometimes—backfire on them.
It's hard to measure "worth" in modern times.
Money buys all. Its power controls the mind.
Being the "best" gets harder every day,
As fourteen billion hands reach out for the same pay.
So, what's it worth to build a great big fire?
If you answered, "Twelve young lives",
Then you're a liar.

That Blaze Of Light

A Poem For Blaze, Who Died So Young

They named him Blaze—and rightly so—
He was a *blaze of light.*
The *moths* came to him in all forms,
And fluttered day and night.
He never burned them with his heat—
Just warmed them, and adorned.
Designing clothes became his dream,
But, now, that dream's been torn.
The girls and friends were bountiful.
He lived a "fast lane" life.
Good looks, good times, and easy cash
Made a life of little strife.
A silver spoon lay in his hand—
A gift his parents gave.
It opened many doors for him….
Alas…, it could not *save.*
His friends—so young and beautiful—
Came, dressed in his designs.
He'd loved them, dressed them, weaved them dreams.
They came to say good-bye.
His mother spoke of who he was,
And how she loved him so.
His father stood with empty eyes
That *stared,* but did not *know.*
He stood, so long at casket's side—
His hand upon the edge….
Life's *meaning* fading fast away,
And, in its place, Life's *dread.*
I wondered, as he stood so long,
What thoughts went through his head.
I think he just *could not let go,*
Even though his son was dead.

The Day The Luck Ran Out

A Poem For Carlos Anaya

"Living on the edge".... It gave him life....
And, then, took it away.
Carlito was the truest friend.
We buried him today.
Through all the years, he had *played* at Life.
He liked to play it *hard.*
He took the dares.... He made the bets.
He played with all his cards.
And he made friends—forever true—
Because of who he was.
He'd lend a hand, *offer* a smile,
Help *banish* tears with love.
And, then...alas...in dead of night,
With all his friends about,
Another game of *dare* he played,
But, *this time,*
His luck ran out.
One hundred fifty thousand volts
Lay waiting for a slip,
And, as he swung across the bar,
His body took the hit.
We watched in horror, as he fell—
His *life* slipping away.
A hand reached out—he squeezed it once.
Death won the game that day.
Now he must live in memories—
The breath of Life snuffed out.
So many hearts will hold him dear—
This...you must never doubt.

Oh How She Danced

A Poem For Sue Roth

Our darling daughter died last night.
She woke to say "good-bye".
Her struggle and her earthly life—
Surcease—without a sigh.
The days before her death…so sad…
Frail steps--filled with such pain.
We wondered…should we let her go,
Or beg her to remain?
It's *hard* to *find* strength to trudge on,
For, no comfort can be found…
When cancer steals a child away,
And lays her in the ground.
Five children blessed us with their lives.
Each one had his own soul—
Two boys…three girls…not one alike…
Striving for different goals.
And so it was…we gathered 'round
To hold a frail, frail hand,
Kiss a pale cheek, stroke tangled hair,
And *wonder*…by whose command…
That she was taken—still so young—
Without a fighting chance.
She so loved life and all living things….
And with each one…she *danced*.

One of the "good ole boys…"
Or *was* he…? YOU decide….
He took a child,
And, for his pleasure,
Splayed him open…wide.
He made him submit…
To secret sodomy—
By day…a coach, a friend,
By night…a *fiend.*
But what of this child,
Who uttered *not a word*…
Pressed into iniquity
By one who *seemed* so good?
How could he speak
Against this saint-like man?
And who would listen?
Who would lend their hand?
His folks—too distant…
His brother—too unkind.
No one to turn to,
No savior could he find.
And…so…he had to be
His own best friend—
Tried to forgive himself
Time and again.
He did not know
That it was not his fault—
His soul o'erburdened, And such pain in his heart.
And, then, the hideous acts…
At *last*…began to fade away.
So, *this* child's soul could breathe again,
And know the light of day.
It *could* have changed this quiet child

Into a deadly fiend.
Instead, it made a gentler soul
Than I have ever seen.
The terror finally went away,
But its *power* never did.
It shaped and sculpted out the man,
And the life he was to live.
A child—so humbled, scarred, and torn—
Branded with such a brand—
From such a child, with such a past,
Would grow what kind of man?
Oh, would it be a twisted brute,
A *bully*…half-insane? Oh…no…*indeed!*
From this crushed psyche
A gentle being came.
He's *been* the world's *best friend*…and *mine*…,
But…still…unto *this* day…
It's hard for him to ever *speak*
The words he needs to say….

I watched my sister "drift" to Death,
Though "drift" is not the word.
The dignity went *days* ago,
Then, care for things of Earth.
She ate one bite at every meal,
Then could not eat at all.
Her eyes grew hollower than her cheeks.
Her frame was skin and bones.
Armed with a diaper—a catheter, too,
She looked Death in the eye.
But Life had other plans for her,
And would not let her die.
A drop of water for dry, parched lips,
A *rub* for cold, cold hands.
As Death drew near, the family watched o'er
This soul…now *stripped* of dreams and plans.
Yes, Life takes back the gifts It's given.
Life takes them…one by one.
She could not move or lift her head.
She could not use her tongue.
Her strength was used to fill her lungs.
All *else* was shutting down.
Her eyes were blank behind closed lids,
Nor could she hear a sound.
Life saved for her the *worst* 'til last—
Plucked every gift It gave her.
She'd prayed for Death some days ago.
She knew only Death could *save* her.
My sister wasn't *afraid* of Death.
She didn't see the *reason*.
She didn't think Hamlet's "dreams" would come—
Just *peace* through all the seasons.
I've often thought the "FAITHFUL'S" "Better Place"

Is something they don't *believe* in.
Why *else* would they all *fear* it so,
And cling to Life with pain—past *reason?*
We *fight* to stay upon this earth,
So Life gives us a *beating*.
Then, Death seems not so *fearsome* a foe
At the end of Life…so *fleeting*.

Justice...Indeed...Is Blind

A Poem For Felix Starr Law

He was the apple of his mama's eye—
Excelled in everything he ever did.
A track star, brilliant student, trusted friend.
He *played* with Life, and It played *back* again.
He was my lover, first, and, then, my friend—
So many happy days of fun and games.
His friends from high school made a *close-knit* band.
They laughed and drank and skied, and life was grand.
He was a *genius* in the insurance game.
He saved his employers *millions*, if not *more*.
They never, *ever* paid him for his worth.
And, then, a high-maintenance *wife*...became his curse.
He spent more than he earned to keep her there.
He gave her child his heart and all his love.
She was a *trophy* wife—*spectacular*!
And, yet, whate'er he gave was not enough.
He deemed it *wrong* to pad "expense accounts"—
The way that his *coworkers* "got around".
Instead, he wrote checks to his wife's account.
Because of *her*, he was caught with *his* pants *down*....
The "insurance" lawyers—lame as they could be—
Made tangled webs he'd have to straighten out.
While they made *millions* for their shoddy work,
He got a paltry sum—not *near* his worth.
And...so...he took his "worth" outside the law.
And...so... "the law" became a guillotine.
His head went rolling—only...I...shed a tear.
His wife *distanced* herself...deemed him "unclean".
The company required that he return it all,
But...LIED...and *reported* it as his *"earned"* pay.
The *deadly* IRS came *after* him.
It cares not whom it maims and whom it slays.

The ruthless IRS garnished *most* of his wage.
He tried to fight *alone,* tried to explain.
The IRS is deadlier than any plague.
It does not care what tragedies are made.
Time and again he'd find a friendly ear,
Who'd *understand* he didn't really owe.
Time and again, that IRS clerk would "disappear".
He felt that he had just one way to go.
So, he made his money in entrepreneurial ways…
Below the radar…worked hard every day.
Cigarettes from Mexico, freon for older cars.
Not *one* thing *bad,* but still "against the law".
His life was good. He treated well his friends.
His parents—grown old--he was so good to them.
He spent his money, time, and patience, too.
He loved them so, there was nothing he wouldn't do.
His luck ran out—the EPA set up a "sting",
Told him *lies* wherein no *truth* did *ever* ring.
They laughed at him as they destroyed his life,
Then drove in fancy cars to homes and wives.
I bailed him out of jail—he was undone.
Too proud to ask for help, this wayward son.
He did not tell his friends what had occurred.
He wrestled his devils…spoke not a single word.
I wonder how it is…some money's made
In "legal" but quite *underhanded* ways.
Like his brother's *lawsuit* against the public schools…
Because his son "fell short" within its rules.
To me, Fe's deeds seemed *philanthropical.*
Through *him* poor Mexicans bought their families… homes.
Through *him* poor Americans had "air" in *older* cars.
Through *him* Big Tobacco's victims *weren't* overcharged.
The "Law" is blind—*there* is no Justice there.
It cuts and slices…limbs…from bodies tears.
The criminals go free. The *good* ones *pay.*
One sees it in our courtrooms every day.

And, so it is, what's "lawful" is, ofttimes, *wrong,*
And things "outside the law" are, ofttimes, *right.*
Our government is *self-serving*…ponderous.
Lays its useless weight on its citizens…breaks trust.
Fe's dad was gone—
But his mother loved him so.
To save him, to the cliff's edge she would go.
He was too proud to tell her of his plight.
He would not be convinced it was *alright.*
Now destitute—the government stole it all—
He *went* 'round to his friends—he *made* the *calls*!
They all thought that he had *gambled* it away.
They would not help or give him time of day.
Guess they'd forgotten those golden days of yore,
When he'd played *generous* host, bought drinks, and *more.*
His stoic silence hid from them…the *truth.*
So they believed what they believed, forsooth.
And, so, he came around to me…his friend.
I borrowed the money…gave it to him, once again.
He thought he could *bail out* and make a score.
But his Mexican connection shut the door.
They must have taken the money…but…no *freon* gave.
He waited in his dilapidated car in lonely desert place.
He must have waited *long.* They never *came.*
Upon himself, alone, he placed the blame.
The money gone. The Adonis in disgrace.
The gold.…long tarnished. The light…gone from his face.
With, Pal, his loyal dog, there, at his side…
They breathed the carbon monoxide. Then they died.
I bit my tongue…kept my true thoughts inside
At the funeral, where the tears mixed with the lies
Of how he'd *gambled* his promising life away.
The piper's tune was way off-key that day.
Fe's last days must have been a Hell on Earth.
The bills…unpaid…*eviction* was his next curse.
In fact, that's how they found the bodies there.

The "evictors" busted the doors into *despair*.
His pride had not *allowed* him to reach out
To his mama, whom he'd honored all his life....
My money gone, I could only give a *home*.
I called and called—no answer on the phone.
For he lay *dead*—his beloved dog, beside...
And all because his Company had lied...
AND because the IRS and EPA didn't care.
They'd set their traps *deep* in their dragons' lairs.
And Justice only sees what She wants to—
Oft blind to what is Just and what is True.
Some call this tragedy a "suicide",
But "murder" seems the word that best describes
The ending of a life that shone so bright.
He gave it up—convinced he'd lost the fight.

Of "Man's Best Friend", Five Kitty Cats, And A Tiger

Wiggly-Waggy Love

A Poem For A Bulldog

Her name was "Dice" 'cause she was black and white.
She never met a man she didn't like.
And, though *men* have bred her *kind* to *love* to fight.
She never thought to use her fearsome bite.
She filled the air with vibrant joy and light.
Her spirit gleamed with wiggly-waggy *might.*
She loved her master…and he loved her, too.
With love that never judged nor e'er was cruel.
They stood *together*—strong against the strife
That always comes as soon as we have life.
She was one great and wiggly burst of love.
And it spilled out all *around* her…and *above.*
Now Death has smothered all her joy and light,
And left in all our hearts the pall of night.
One heart is sadder, still, than all the rest,
For *that* heart loved her *true*…and loved her best.

The Last Good-bye

A Poem For Bruno

'Twas *once* I lived in fear of *any* dog.
I could not help myself. The fear was taught.
And, then, I found a tiny, frisky friend.
Upon his *love* I learned I could depend.
He taught me many things, and I taught him.
The fear that I once had began to dim.
He showed me I could love what…once…I shunned.
And we were best of friends when it was done.
We travelled—he and I—through many years.
We shared the best of times. We shared the tears.
And, then, one day the light went from his eyes.
His movements slowed, his walk—no longer spry.
The doctor gave us hope, so how we tried
To save his life, but we were all denied.
When Death came 'round, we tried to shut Him out.
But Death comes where He will—this—do not doubt.
Before my Bruno died, he said good-bye.
To think of it will ever make me cry.
His tiny paw reached out as if to say,
"If only you could make this pass away.
I love you so, as I have *every* day.
I feel my life is slipping fast away.
Do not forget me, then I'll always be
There…in your heart…
As you were there for me."

"The little one" should not have been—
It seemed so *clear* to me.
Yet…there she was, *trying* to live,
Snuggled up so *close* to me.
Too weak to nurse—too incomplete—
Her *insides* were not right—
A tiny thing who softly moaned,
And could not win the fight.
Life is *painted* by "the Hand of God",
Though Man has been painting, too.
And, when the painting's incomplete,
There's little we can do.
Yet…still…I wonder why God's Hand
Would paint so *carelessly*…,
And give this little one to love,
Then take her *back* from me.

The Grave Upon The Hill

A Poem for "Bear" And Mary Rowan

My best friend *rests*—
For I laid him there—
In the grave upon the hill.
He is sleeping, now,
'Neath his favorite spot
In his grave upon the hill.
Cradled in my arms,
He drew *his last* breath,
As I whispered in his ear,
"Beary, did you know
You've been *my best friend*—
Good and *true*—these sixteen years?"
He just *wagged* his tail,
As he *looked* at me—
Happy to be in my arms.
'Twas the *last* thing he would *ever* know.
Now his soul rests—safe from harm.
I had rescued him when he was a pup
From the *long* arm of the law—
Just a *hyper* little ball of fur,
Running 'round on racetrack sod.
He stayed at *my barn,* guarded *my shed row,*
And, when strangers tried to pass…
They would either have to go *around,*
Or get bitten in the ass.
As the years passed by, we became best friends,
Though his mind worked its own way.
I would try to teach. He would try to learn,
And hold his "devilment" at bay.
Other friends would come. Other friends would go.
But my Beary stayed the same.
He would *sleep* by me whene'er I felt *low*—

Lick my *cheek* when I spoke his name.
But old "Father Time" robs us of our youth—
Leaves us feeble, deaf and blind.
And my willful pup was aging *seven years*
For every *single one* of mine.
He was my beloved. He was my best friend.
He stood by me all those years.
But the bells were tolling…I could hear them toll,
And I knew they tolled for him.
Yet, I did not *want* him travelling *alone…*
To the edge of that dark night.
And I did not *want* him feeling any pain,
Loneliness, or anguished fright.
So, I cradled him in my *bravest* love,
As I held him in my arms,
It was in my arms that he passed to Death—
Never fearing any harm.
Then I carried him to his favorite spot,
Where he'd liked to rest…so still.
Now he sleeps *beneath*—
Nor will ever stir…
From his grave upon the hill.

I saw the vultures *circling* o'er the field,
And thought I'd better see what had been killed.
I found a golden dog—all skin and bone.
She lay there…*dying*…lost and all alone.
I knew that I must save her with all speed.
For Death was fast approaching on His steed.
On steed of Love and Hope we rode that day.
And Death's steed…soon…began to fade away.
My Doc and I fought each ill, as it came.
And, so, she lived, and we gave her a name.
Our "Goldie" bloomed—she scampered, frisked, and played.
I grew to love her more each passing day.
From time to time, I'd look behind to see
If Death still followed on his coal-black steed.
But, it was in the *woods* I should have searched.
Death came upon us—*sudden*—our horse lurched,
And threw us to the ground 'neath thundering hooves.
Then Death leaned down and whispered,
"You've been beaten".
I did not want to *listen*—tried to save
For only *I* stood between *her* and the *grave*.
So we rose up—I held her in my arms.
The doctor tried, once more, to conquer harm.
But she had suffered far too many blows
In her short life, and now they laid her low.
Frantic with hunger, she had eaten rocks—
There, deep inside, they stayed.
Her pups had died within her womb.
It had become their grave.
Inside her, as the time passed by,
The rocks and dead pups *inflamed*.
Voracious cancer devoured her,
As it grew without a name.

The cards that Life had dealt her
Boded Death
Ere she was born…
Or first knew light or breath.
And, so…at last…I had to say good-by.
My arms fell—helpless—as my Goldie died.

The Gardener's Folly

A Poem For "Special"

The gardener came here once a week,
And brought along his crew.
Sometimes his pit-bull came along,
And, sometimes, he'd bring *two*.
I thought he knew my dogs were girls
Who still had *all their parts*.
I thought he knew "boys will be boys",
And *he'd* keep them *apart*.
Alas…so busy pruning shrubs…
I guess he did not hear
The voice of Nature, as She spoke—
Her message *loud and clear!*
Later…our dalmatian disappeared.
We searched the whole day through.
Then, we heard some *scratching* beneath the house
Where we could not fit through.
One pup had *already* been born—
Finally, we coaxed them forth—
A puppy just as black as night—
The *first* of many more.
We named her "Special", because she was.
We did not know her dad
'Til the gardener came back with his dog,
And we knew how we'd been "had".
We found good homes for all the pups,
But we kept "Special" here.
My children said this "Special" pup
Was ours…and that was clear.
The bulldog in her was so strong,
It made her stand apart.
It taught her how to jump a fence,
And how to hunt in dark.

She could scale a six-foot fence with ease.
And…she ate coyotes for lunch.
She was often wary of strange folks,
But she loved my kids a *bunch*.
The neighbor got a brand-new pup,
And she became his friend.
She'd play with him, then steal his toys,
And scale the fence, again.
At first it was a laughing thing.
The toys *went back* each day.
But as the puppy—*bolder*—*grew*
She did not get her way.
And, so, it ended in a fight.
The neighbor screamed and *raved*.
He swore *that* he would *shoot* our dog—
And that *she could not* be saved.
Her spirit was so wild and free,
No fence could keep her in.
The coyotes that she'd fought and killed
Hung around her neck like "sin".
And, so, they called her "killer—vile".
I knew not what to do.
I could not risk the *other* lives,
With bullets passing through.
For I had children, dogs and cats—
And horses—old and new.
He was so hate-crazed, he might take
The others with her, too.
He'd stacked the deck—lied to the cops—
No law would stop him, now.
In fact, the law *empowered* him—
Made *good* his deadly vow.
And, so, I took her in my truck
To have her put to sleep.
The lies, the laws, the insanity
Had laid her at Death's feet.

Because of her *exuberance*,
She'd never gotten "to ride",
So when I told her to "jump in"
Her heart swelled up with pride.
She sat so *proudly* on the seat—
So happy to be *riding*.
She'd wiggle over, and lick my cheek—
Not knowing why we were driving.
Though, *usually,* I can handle Death,
Because I know Him well—
I scarce could breathe…I scarce could see,
As I drove us into Hell….
I hope the last thoughts in her mind
Were not of fear and death,
But that she finally got *to ride*…
And that "Special" means "the *best*".

Science, Technology, And Love

A Poem For "Tech" And Lori

The time has come to let me go.
I know it's hard to do....
You have a shell that's *hard* and *tough,*
But that's not really you.
You saved me many years ago,
When I was just a pup.
The science lab could not use me.
It seemed the jig was up.
But...there you were to save a 'dalmatian'
Whose coat had grown too long
For the lab tests men had planned for me
Behind doors that hid great wrong....
You saved a long-haired cat and me—
Named us "Science" and "Technology",
Convinced ole Roy my spots would come—
Gave the gift of Life to me.
The gift you gave has lasted years.
They've been so full of love—
Of treats, and pats, and fireside glow,
And my place...there...on the rug.
Your sassy horses, and two little girls
Helped wile away my days.
We'd romp and play and run around,
Or climb up on the hay.
And from our spot atop the hay,
We could see for miles around.
The breezes blew, the clouds blew by,
The bright ole sun shone down....
But, now, the Hands of Father Time
Have closed around my throat so *tight,*
I can barely breathe. I can barely walk,
Or tell the day from night.

Each gurgling breath…
I breathe for you—*a labor of my love.*
Each breath I breathe should be my last,
But you just can't let go.
I cling to life by tiny threads,
But I'm not really here….
It's too *hard* for you to *play* "the Hand of God"
When it's a *great love*…standing there….

She Was My Love

A Poem For Fina And Sasha

We met when she was just a pup.
And, then, we fell in love—
A German Shorthaired…bred to hunt,
Who wouldn't hurt a dove.
We watched her grow.
She shared our lives.
She, soon, was one of us.
She greeted us, sat at our feet,
And never made a fuss.
And…she would "point" at butterflies,
Or anything that flew.
Though never *taught*,
Something *inside* her
Told her what to do.
So "still"—she pointed—
Would not budge, or bark, or move,
Or blink an eye.
Instinct was stronger than all *else*—
And all for a *butterfly*.
I think she knew I loved her so—
That she *was* my *special* one—
That she was mine, and I was hers
When all was said and done.
So many years passed by so fast—
Sasha was always there,
With wagging tail and friendly eyes
To lighten my despair.
Then, of a sudden, she was old.
Where had the days all gone?
Though her walk had slowed, her tail still wagged,
Until cancer came along.
The cancer won… My Sasha died….

Too *painful* to tell my friends…
Because…you see…she was *my love,*
And I could not face her end.
There's little left but Father Time
To lessen my despair.
And…still…whene'er I close my eyes.
My Sasha's sitting there.

Just A Little

A Poem For Don And Zip

I thought I loved him—just a *little*—
Knew not my life…around him grew.
I thought I'd miss him—just a little.
But I was wrong about that…, too.
His tiny frame—inconsequential.
His tiny paws scarce left a mark.
But, when Death's fury swept down on him,
His loss hurled lightness into dark.
He treated me like someone special.
He looked to me for *everything.*
Content whene'er he could be near me.…
A strong bond grew like flowers in the spring.
We woke up *early,* just as always.
The park we loved—just down the lane.
But—there—*outside,* a pit bull waited
To carry my Zipper to his grave.
I ran, with all my might, to save him,
To wrest him from the jaws of death.…
Too *great* the damage when I *found* him.
All that remained was his *last breath.*
My life seems to have *lost* its *structure.*
My heart has lost its truest friend.
My mind seeks solace, as it wonders
Why Fate dealt out this fearsome end.

George
A Hero,
If There Ever Was One.

When "Small" Is Just Another Word

A Poem for George—Manaia, New Zealand's
Jack Russell Terrier

His little body lies at rest—
So tattered and so torn.
Just yesterday he ran and played—
Nor did the signs forewarn.
But, as he jumped, *frolicked* and played—
Welcomed "his kids" from town,
A *bloodlust* of Man's *own* design
Came bounding o'er the ground.
Two pit bulls—bred from Man's desire
For power and savagery—
Attacked the children as they played—
Death seemed a *certainty*.
Just then, a knight stood, with no shield—
No armor of shining steel.
He used his body… his courage…his love—
And all his strength of will.
He saved his little friends that day,
But paid a mighty price.
He made the trade, And for their sakes,
He offered up his life….

Lucy with Her Ashley

You were my friend…the best of all. I had to leave you there.
You stood by me through darkest pall. I had to leave you there.
You never asked too much of me, but you were always there.…
We shared so many, many years. And then I left you there.
The cancer grew. I did not know, and you did not complain.
The doctor said, "Now, let her go. There's nothing left but pain".
I held you…whispered *how I loved,* though you could barely hear.
I held you, hoping that my arms would help allay your fear.
One instant passed…from life to death…the journey had been made.
The specter drug had done its work. Now…nothing…but the grave.
You looked so *small*…so helpless…*still.* It seemed too much to bear.
One last good-bye, and one last glance…and then I left you there.
I wrote these words when, first, we met. Now they come back to me.…
Such *simple* words to have the strength to bind our destinies.…
"I'm taking the puppy, if only to teach her some manners.
I'll bring her back if you want me to, or if it doesn't work out."
I guess it worked.… For fifteen years, my Lucy-dog was here.
The cancer grew…I helped her die, then had to *leave* her *there.*
The cancer grew…I helped her die…, then had to leave her…there.…

Waylon and his Kids

We Walked Through Fields Of Gold

A Poem For Our Golden Retriever, Waylon…Most Beloved

A golden retriever…extraordinaire!
Not one could brighter shine.
So full of courage, full of love—
Wise eyes that were so kind.
He was my husband's dog, at first,
But, then, I called him *mine*.
The kids were born. His mission was…
To keep them both from harm.
I "strollered" them 'round the neighborhood,
And up into the hills.
With him along, I never feared
We'd ever meet any ill.
When friendly neighbors came up to chat,
He'd quietly sit *down*
Between them and the kids he loved,
Nor growl or make a sound.
He let the kids crawl over him,
And pull his ears and tail.
They'd hug him with their chubby arms,
And kiss him *everywhere*.
When Springtime came, he'd think of *love*—
A-bounding he would go.
And every "fair maiden" in our hills
Would a "maiden" be no more.
We moved "uptown" to homes of dreams,
Built by *Newhall* Land And Farm.
We did the soccer, gymnastics, T-ball…
Honed our social skills and charms.
My "fancy" turned to raising horses,
My husband's fancy turned *away*
To the pretty girls at CBS,
Where he spent his working days.

And when he *left* us, Waylon *stayed*
With his *true* family.
His quiet courage, quiet love
Shown out for all to see.
I was so busy as a single mom,
I *missed* the fact that he…
Had grown so old, and suffered pain
From "old dog" maladies.
The vet found cancer on his hip—
Stretched him out for x-rays and tests.
He could not walk when I picked him up.
All he *wanted* was to rest.
I'd set him down and leave for work.
There he'd be when I got home.
He couldn't move *even an inch.*
He was fur and skin and bone.
That Friday night, I slept by him
Under a tree in our front yard,
For Saturday would be his last.
Life had dealt the final card.
I carried him to our old vet.
I held him in my arms.
His eyes had lost all of their light.
For peace his body longed….
Years later, the husband who had left us all
Told me a *startling* thing.
He thought I'd put this great love down
Only to bring him pain.
For, you see, upon *that very day,*
He'd taken a pretty, young bride.
He thought that it was for…*revenge*
My Waylon had to die.
I guess he'd known me NOT AT ALL
In all those years gone by,
If he *really* thought…to cause *him* pain
I'd make this *great love*…die.

I kept my horses at Luanne's.
She owned a "Mac Donald's Farm"…
With horses, geese, pigs, cats and dogs…
Paddocks, pens, and barns.
Her dalmatian kept on getting bred.
Her springer was the cad.
A dozen puppies came from it.
We can't say we were *glad*.
We could not find homes for all of them,
So I took one with me.
I named her Lisa. She fit in….
The rest is destiny.
She romped and played with Ash and Stu—
My little girl and boy.
She made *best friends* of our two dogs—
A household filled with joy.
When Lucy died, Liza was there.
She helped to ease the pain.
She was the *matron* from then on,
Through dogs and cats and years.
The day I had to let her go, the doctor came to me.
Her organs all were shutting down.
She was so old, you see.
So sad…on our dining table…there—
Sweet Lisa drew a breath,
Then whimpered as the drug set in—
And gave way to sleep of Death.

The most *unloved* of our four dogs—
That was to be her fate.
Perhaps we loved her *just enough*
To…*mostly*…fill her plate.
She *tried* to be so *lovable*.
She tried so to fit in.
The bulldog *sometimes* fought with her,
And…never…did she win.
When I leaned down to pat her head,
My poor toes she would nail…
By *accident*…with her front paws,
From her frantic joy—uncurtailed.
My little Ren, our chihuahua pup,
Got plugged up by a bone.
Sidetracked—the vet *forsook* my Ren,
And left him to die…alone.
That was Punky's last day, too.
She could no longer stand.
I sat in the vet's exam room,
With both my dogs laid out.
One…the victim of Father Time…
The other of a rookie and
Distracted vet, no doubt.

When Small Is Big

A Poem For Little Ren

My mighty dog is *mighty*. On *that* you can depend.
His *real* name's Alexander, but we just call him "Ren".
He shares home with four other dogs,
Aged one...six...nine...thirteen.
He's friendly with the three old souls,
But to the pup, he's mean.
Although the pup's a bulldog,
And fifteen times his size,
She hangs her head, all meek and mild,
When he looks her in the eyes.
He goes a-riding in our car
To see what he can see,
And when he sees a Taco Bell,
That's where he wants to be.
He loves to cruise the neighborhood.
He visits with his friends.
The neighbors stopped returning him.
Now, they just ask him in.
He visits here...he visits there.
He loves to make his rounds.
But...always...when the nighttime comes,
He's sleeping, safe and sound,
Beneath the covers on my bed,
Curled up so *snug-gl-y*,
And dreaming dreams of Taco Bell,
And how he's loved by me.

I got her to be Stuey's pup.
Then...*somehow*...she was *mine*.
The *kids* named her for "smokin' weed".
The name "Mary Jane" seemed fine.
She was the fourth dog in our home.
We shared the moments—all.
She watched the kids grow up and fly,
And her three friends beneath Death's hand fall.
She watched me struggle mightily
To pull the weight alone.
For...then, it was just she and I,
With all the others gone.
The years passed by, and she was there
To greet, forgive, and love.
But Father Time gives so few years
To animals Man so loves.
Her body---worn. Her time had come.
She quietly left this earth.
There are no words that I can say...
That could describe her worth.

Oh, he was such a bounding soul.
But he had so little time.
He gave his love to Ann and me
From heart—rambunctious…kind.
A fiery ball of energy,
A brawny ball of might.
He had the strength to fly through space,
Catch frisbees in their flight.
Old Mary Jane put up with him.
Dear Roxie thought him "keen".
The "burdies" weren't afraid of him.
They knew he wasn't mean.
He'd lick my face, sleep on my chest,
And follow me around.
He'd take the stairs without a dare,
Sometimes in a single bound.
Then, of a sudden, he was sick.
He whimpered, stumbled, fell….
And Annie had to watch him die
That day that came from Hell.
The autopsy revealed the truth
That solved the mystery.
His *bounding* might *twisted* his gut,
And stole his light from me.

Little Min....

A Poem For Ashley's Pup

Just *three* inches tall—black as *any* night—
Is my precious little Min.
Only *half* the size of her littermates…,
Oh, but could she "do them in".
And the tiny heart that beats *within*
Her *minute* chihuahua frame…
Knows not any fear, knows not any "mean",
Knows not any "wimpiness" or blame.
Minnie weighs just above a pound…views the world *close to the ground.*
She has round, liquid eyes…a tongue that *greets,*
And a "savy" that astounds.
Yes, she knows to "go" where the going is good.
Never "goes" upon the *rug.*
Folks can't figure out if she's a *dog*
Or a hamster, a *mouse,* or a bug.
Since they can't be sure, and don't want to be *wrong,*
They just scratch their heads and grin.
"That's the *tiniest* 'animal' I have ever seen!"
"No…*EXCUSE* me, that's my darling Min!"
Little Min is "smawrt". She has spunk and spark.
When she likes the food, she'll eat.
Then her belly swells up bigger than her head,
And she wobbles on her tiny feet.
Little Minnie…now…is passing ten weeks old,
And I've called her *mine* for two.
She's brought Spring's *bright* bloom, and *lightened* my life
With her three inches of "five-feet-two".

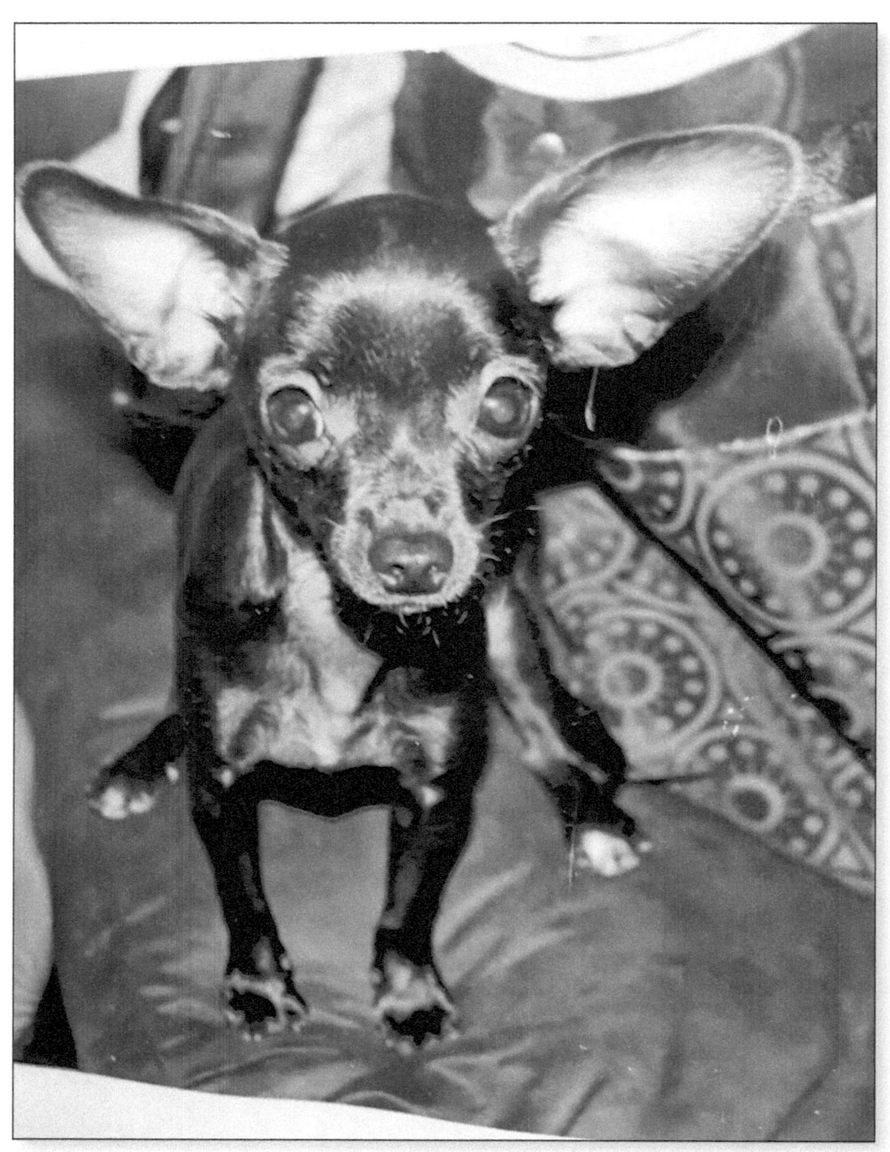

Our *first* encounters were of the *wary* sort.
He was the big and *silent* type.
I thought he'd "claw" for sport,
But he'd just lie there,
Sprawled out on my knees.
He let me know that's where he wished to be.
And so it was that we became fast friends.
He'd *visit* me, and…*stay* time and again.
Some playful kids had named him *"Catillac"*.
And he preferred my touch, and "dug" my *digs*.
I finally learned his name was really "Hobbs",
And, though a *cat,* he *loved* more like a dog.
When his owners *moved,* I thought they'd take him, too.
But they said, "No—seems he belongs to you".
The time passed by…so *quickly*—all content.
And, then, the cancer came—the good times went.
We fought against it—he, the doc, and I…no cost too great—
Nothing we would not try.
But Death comes 'round in spite of all you do.
And leaves with what you loved—so deeply—so true….

A Poem For "Little Man" And Missy

A litter of kittens—"What to do?"
My friend, Satui, asked me.
I'll give you four, and keep the rest.
You find them *homes*. You do your best.
Our *"best" we did*. We found two homes.
We kept the *other* two.
One disappeared within a year. Her fate we never knew.
And that left one—black as the night,
And not the friendly type
We named her "Missy", fed her well,
And *avoided* her "warning" bites.
Then Mario came to break our horses.
Two bobtail cats came with him.
One of them...soon... went on his way.
One *stayed* to do our *mice* in.
He stayed to himself. He lived outside.
The *mice* on our ranch *feared* him.
He ate the food that we put out,
But wouldn't let us near him.
Finally, one day, he wanted friends,
So Lee and I *obliged* him.
A "family", of sorts, was *finally* formed—
Two misfit cats...two ranchers.
He *sprayed*. She spat. We built our ranch—
Each post and tree and fence line.
Our two black cats kept mice at bay...
Other critters we had-- of ALL kinds.
The peacocks, roosters, laying hens,
The pigeons, goats and quail,
Sometimes, a wandering pig or two...
Of our *hospitality* did avail.
The cougars, hawks and ravens dined

Upon our menagerie.
The coyotes came…snakes slithered by,
As we made *history*.
We named out bobtail "Little Man",
For he *wasn't* very *big*.
He was big in *presence*…courage, too.
And he *sure could* be a *prig!*
Our "Little Man" was the first to go.
He got so very thin.
We found him stretched out on the floor—
So little left of him.
Soon Missy followed in his steps.
She, too, wasted away.
She went from *fulsome* flesh to frail—
Her *kidneys* had given way.
They both were "mousers" to the end.
They *tolerated* us.
We think they actually loved us, too,
Though they never made a fuss.

Monkeyshine And Snowball

The Twin Tornados Of San Lee Ranch

A Calico with…no white at all—
A *wiry* little thing!
A tempest in a teapot…*sure*…
With *horns,* not angel wings….
We found him…trackside…on the hay—
White as the driven snow—
Stretched out and napping *without mom.*
He was… "grown up", you know.
We brought him home to be her pal.
At first, they hissed and spat.
She'd *whack* him one, then run away.
But, *always*, she'd come back.
My legs, in jeans, just seemed to be
Her favorite things to climb.
So up and down them she would go,
As if I didn't mind.
They made the wind whirl when they played—
That twin-tornado pair.
'Twas up and down curtains and beds….
They could tip a *rocking* chair.
Each had some thoughts about our dogs…
One ran, one just *ignored.*
We'd watch their antics—laugh a lot—
A "show" that never bored….
They caught a mouse the other day—
A *most important* thing.
They had *practiced* on their favorite toy—
A *stuffed mouse* on a string….
They've brought *new life* into our home
That's seen sad, stressful times.
When we feel low, we watch them play.
It helps us keep our minds.

A Tiger's Tale

The Story Of The Moorpark Tiger

Not ever taught to hunt or kill,
Or have to make his way.
He lived his life as someone's pet,
And then he slipped away.
He wandered…lost…amongst the hills,
Not knowing what to do.
His clawless paws left telltale signs
That something was askew.
As scores of people searched for him,
A bitter hunger gnawed.
It had him in its clutches…there…
When the rifles brought him down.
He never hurt a single soul.
He never used his power.…
To kill never occurred to him,
Even in his final hour.…

9

Of Horses and the People Who Love Them

Closing Doors

A Poem For Beth's Beloved Pinto, Sham

The doors keep on a-closing
As I travel through my life.
And there will be no *turning back.*
Waste not the tears and strife.
This last door was the hardest, yet,
Because it took away
A friend who *had* been good and true,
And loved me every day.
I tried to *hold* him…*keep* him here.
I tried to make him stay.
But love has lost, and Death has won.
My Sham is gone away.
Yet, in my heart, he'll always *stay*
As long as I draw breath…
Until the last door closes…
That lays me to my rest.

Christopher...When Thirty Years Is Not Enough

A Poem For Pam And Her Beloved Chris

He was *just four months,* and I was twenty-one *years*…
When…I…became his "mom".
A dapple gray whose roots stretched back
To Arabian sands and sun.
At first, with cautious *baby steps,*
He'd slowly come to me.
His velvet, whiskered baby nose—
Brave…with shy curiosity.
And we became the best of friends—
He'd always count on me.
And I would always *count* on him—
That's *what* friends do, you see.
I named him *Chris.* I trained him *well.*
He did just what I asked.
Team Penning was his great forte,
But he shone in every class.
We rode together thirty years,
Shared many ribbons—blue.
The circles of our lives *entwined.*
And he was ever true.
Then Father Time, Who comes to call,
No matter what we do—
Began to take the gifts He gave,
As He made way for the new.
A temperature and failing flesh,
And then a valiant fight,
As Chris, Doc Looper, Forrest and I
Fought back with all our might.
And just when we thought that we had won…
At least a few more years,
Dark Death rode up on his black horse—
Filled our respite with tears.

We called two vets—begged them to come—
For Looper was out of town.
We needed them to ease his pain,
But they both turned us down.
So…left without their specter drug
To ease his way to death,
Chris had to walk a path of pain,
And suffer great distress.
We walked *beside*—Forrest and I—
Chris whinnied from the pain.
With vital organs shutting down,
He collapsed beneath the strain.
His eyes *beseeched*. His body *twitched*.
His insides blew apart,
As he lay there in our helpless arms,
The light gave way to dark.
We buried him beneath the ground,
Now hallowed by the love
That grew between a little foal
And a girl of twenty-one.

My Goldie

Li'l Goldie was my *pony*. Oh, I did love her so.
She took me here. She took me there.
We always stole the show.
We travelled many, many miles—
My mommy, she and I,
She always took good care of me,
And never made me cry.
She jumped, she cantered, trotted, walked.
She did the things I asked.
She *always* helped me with her skill,
And kept me to my task.
Then…suddenly…she could not trot,
She could not walk or run….
And, so, we called the doctor in
To see what could be done.
We tried so hard…for many days
To stop what hurt her so.
Then, deep inside, we found a stone
That had no place to go.
The doctor made one last attempt
To save my Goldie's life.
But we had found the stone too late.
It was then my Goldie died.
I hope that, *somehow*, she still knows
I love her *tenderly*,
And that I'll hold her in my heart,
And keep her…here…with me.

I was not sure when he was born,
Or just how *old* he *was*.
I knew he'd spent too many years
Riding in those rodeo wars.
Kids—barrel racing or roping calves—
Called on his strength and speed.
He gave 'til there was little left—
Fulfilled their every need.
We bought him, tired and all worn out.
We brought him back to life.
With love and care, our Sammy *bloomed*—
Forgot the rodeo strife.
And he became my show pony—
His *prowess* soon *renowned*.
He trotted, cantered, jumped for me.
Blue ribbons showered down.
My sister always called him *"orange"*.
I guess he *might* have been—
With speckles and a crazy mane—
And hooves turned out way more than in.
I grew to love him…and he loved me.
He showed his love each day.
My mom and Sam taught me new skills.
Their patience lit my way.
We were a team—*unbeatable*,
And we swept all the shows.
On points and ribbons—so far in front—
The gap could not be closed.
But those old "wars" left silent wounds
That smoldered deep inside.
And…one day…those old wounds flared up.
So came my Sam's last ride.
My mommy did the best she could

To find what caused his pain.
No test…no vet…could find the key
To make him young, again.
We gave him things to ease the pain,
But his pain just grew and grew.
At last, I said I'd let him go.
'Twas best for him, I knew.
And Death rode up on His great horse,
As I went off to school….
My mommy says Sam taught me best.
What mommy says is true.

Kristilar's Legacy

A Poem For Carole's Beloved Mare

She tried to catch the *wind* each time she raced…
Her body strong, determined, full of grace.
But it is *seldom* one can catch the wind.
The wind is *fickle*—can be foe or friend.
Sometimes it blew *beneath* or at her back.
Sometimes it raged against her on the track.
For years I loved her, and she carried me.
She made the dreams I dreamt…*reality.*
But now the time has come to let her rest.
Each time I asked, she always gave her best.
Each time she raced, she raced with heart and soul,
Her body…getting weary, growing old.
Now—tables turned—'tis she who asks of me
To do my best to fill her destiny
With happy days and babies that can run,
And, maybe, catch the wind when it is done.

A burnished chestnut—bound to be a gray.
Too *big*, too *early*—she was born that day.
I loved her at *first sight*—a *sight* she *was!*
A *sight* not even her *own mother* loved.
We battled weakened ankles—fragile bones.
The Doc and I…together…fought *alone.*
For Nature never *lent* us Her *strong arm.*
And Nature never kept this foal from harm.
Instead, Nature *betrayed* Her precious child.
A fairy's tale was told—the fairy lied.
Her bones began to *shatter,* one by one…
No strength in them—her life was all undone.
And so I had to bid my foal *adieu.*
Her life of pain and strife so quickly through.
She had so little time to sing her song,
So, I will sing it for her my life long.

He came into this world of ours one dark and frantic night—
Ripped from his mother's womb in a birth
That filled him with such fright.
His mother did not know her foal, and soon cast him aside.
A kindly lady came to save, and raised him at her side.
He never learned his *manners* well, so he grew very *bold.*
He soon became *incorrigible,* if truth were to be told.
Fortune, again, abandoned him, and looked the other way.
And so, his leg began to grow more crooked every day.
His destiny, forever *changed*—for he would never race,
Nor carry on his grandsire's name, his legend or his grace.
But *somewhere,* there…along the way…
He'd learned how to be *kind.*
And, so, armed with this precious gift,
His place he sought to find.
And then, one day a young girl came,
And looked into his eyes,
And, in them, thought she saw a friend
Who *could* not be disguised.
She welcomed him into her life,
And *he welcomed* her, too.
With every day that passed them by,
Their friendship grew and grew.
Then Fortune, jealous of this bliss,
When…next…She looked his way,
Decided it was not to be,
And, so, took him away.
He caught his halter on the fence,
Then struggled *mightily.*
His struggles caught the eye of Death—
Only his soul went free.
Oh, *cruel* it was to take him thus,
And so bizarre…the way.

His path upon this earth—star-crossed—
From birth to his last day.
So brief his life…so sad his end….
And we are all dismayed!
What God is this Who would so *treat*
A creature that he *made?*

Beware...Lest The Smell Of Fear
Awakens Death From Out His Slumber

Star-crossed, then crossed again…kept from the sun.
The die was cast before the race was run.
I did not *heed* the warning in the stars,
Nor, at her birth, bells tolling near and far.
I named her for my dad, whom I loved so.
I thought that, from this love, *blessings* would flow.
But not a blessing did I ever see.
The night her son was born, she turned on me—
Turned on him, too…so he was raised alone—
Without a mother he could call his own.
And then, he died before he e'er turned two.
A broken neck left nothing left to do.
A daughter born...within hid tragic flaw,
Whose power, ever growing…*again*…spewed out the law.
So, this foal, too died young, by her own hand.
When stars are crossed, 'tis *heaven* dictates the plan.
Another daughter born, by sire renowned.
But, deep within, the tragic flaw was found.
What is this flaw that rules *despotically?*
Their souls—in stress—lose their *stability.*
Their souls—in stress *frantic* to get away…
Fight dragons never seen by night or day.
Invisible…these dragons took them all—
Two foals…their dam succumbed to Death's black pall.
And now, two daughters left, but who's to say
When dark of night will fall and crush the day?

What happened to my sweet Diana B—
That silly little filly named for me.
It seems she was just here, but now she's gone.
The time that she was given wasn't long.
She came into this world one wintry night—
A bundle far too small…still…mom's delight.
But only mommy loved her for a while,
Nor did she ever know a human smile.
Her mommy taught her not to trust in men.
So it was hard to win her heart, again.
And, Fate, ever playing *games,* just took the "bone"
Out of her feet, then Fate left her alone…
Just long enough to find a place to be,
Where love could finally bring *serenity.*
'Twas to this place a family came one day…
To find a horse with whom their horse could play.
Some way they *knew,* when looking in her eyes,
The thing they *saw* was frightened LOVE *disguised.*
They made a place for her—there—in their hearts.
But on the day that she was to depart,
Fate once again stepped in and thundered,
"Nay! Diana will not find a new life today…."
Instead, Fate took her…there…before our eyes,
And gave her unto Death,
To be His prize.

Ashley and Stuey with their new friend "Tolley"

The bell has tolled, and called him *home,*
Soon it will toll for me.
What force decrees when it will toll
Remains a mystery.
I watched him come into this world,
Walked with him through the years—
The *last* foal from a mare I loved.
Her death brought many tears.
He grew up handsome—grew up kind.
He grew up without fear.
A child could lie down next to him—
SAFE—with his power near.
But, under saddle, people found
He was a "bouncy" boy—
Too "bouncy" ever to win a race.
Yet…still…my pride and joy.
And, so, I brought him home, again,
To *always* be with me—
This last son of the mare I loved,
Whose soul had long roamed free.
Too "bouncy", still, for me to ride,
I wondered what to do—
My hours all spent *dealing* with Life,
Dire straits, teenagers, too.
My "Luck" had *long ago* run out,
And now lives in South of France.
My partners *since*—Malaise and Mishap—
Twirl me in breathless dance.
He must have wondered where I was, and why I only came
But once a week to give a *hug,* a *carrot,* and call his name.
My good friend, Lori, cared for him, and turned him out to play.
She knew him well, had such insight…
Was never far away,

He seemed a little *off his feed.* He was not *acting* right.
We thought that it was just a "bug".
But *Death* set up *this* fight.
And, so, we called the Doctor in.
He said, "It's all in vain.
Sure death is waiting at day's *end.*
The pathway's paved with pain".
And, so, they led him to the hill,
Where a wind so often blows,
They gave his body unto Death,
The *wind* caught up his *soul.*
I never got to say good-bye—
See *last light* in his eyes,
Or throw my arms around his neck,
My cheek pressed to his side.
I *thought* that I could hold him safe,
I asked not for whom bells toll—
That warning, penned by Hemingway—
Echoes from long ago.
But even though I never *asked,*
The bell tolled deafeningly.
Its peals *silenced* "For Thee It Tolls",
Rang out, "It tolls for thee".

Rosey's Posy

A Poem For Ra Ra Rose And Her Foal

Our Rosey had her "posy". But only for a *while.*
It *seemed* the sun shone down on us,
But Death hid behind that smile.
Rosey's filly was a *great gift given* to a mare long past her prime,
Old mares ofttimes do not produce
A *grand* foal of this kind.
But, somewhere in the sandy soil,
Or in her mother's womb—bacilli *lay in wait*
To turn her "light" to dismal gloom.
She frolicked, nursed, then *peaked* at us
From behind mom's shoulder—strong.
It seemed this little one was blessed, and nothing would go wrong.
Naïve—we did not know that day that, with her first drawn breaths,
Bacilli—fearsome, insidious—began *drowning* her in death.
The blood spewed out. *Organs* gave way.
The toxins gripped her brain.
The doctor helped as best he could
To keep her from the pain.
And as the *hours* slipped *away,*
So did her chance at life.
We wondered how Fate chose the souls
Who must be *sacrificed....*

Lady-In-Waiting

In Remembrance Of "Lady"

Her *full* name was "Stalwart's Bay Lady".
She was *born* of a sire most renowned.
So, I *always* expected more of her—
Wanted her to be more than I found.
She was pretty, but a little club footed.
She was smallish—a little back-at-the-knee.
Her grown *babies* hadn't run worth a *nickel*—
Not the *stuff* that makes dreams *"history"*.
In the pasture, her place was "the *bottom*"—
Always *picked* on by the mares "above".
She was chased off the hay and the carrots—
Never finding a "pal" who would love.
At the sale it was…I…who had bought her—
Proud I was 'til my friends showed her flaws.
She'd been shiny and polished and sturdy.
And I bid all I had…without pause.
What seems shiny and polished can get tarnished.
What seems gallant and grand may not be.
And *the best of the best*…may not even be enough.
Life's so full of *illusions,* you see.
In spite of it all, I still loved her,
Though she never knew it, I guess….
I would throw her a handful of carrots
In a spot far away from the rest.
Sometimes…she would have time to eat them.
Sometimes…she would be driven off.
Sometimes…she'd be kicked by the *boss* mares.
Living life on the *fringe*—I guess *that* was her cross.
Still—she gave me one good-looking baby,
And she carried another inside.
She accepted her place at the *bottom*.
Watching her would, *sometimes,* make me cry.

For it's *hard* to be nobody's favorite.
And it's *hard* to be nobody's friend.
And it's *hard* to be just *mediocre,*
And then die…all alone…at the end.
So unloved, even *Nature* forsook her—
Lame and sweating, with her foal trapped *inside*—
Complications *beyond* understanding—
In a paddock…alone…they both died.

The Last Dance

A Poem For My Beloved Dollar A Dance

I met a man who was no man at *all*—
A scoundrel through and through, his spirit…*small*.
He sold me an old mare he thought was "done".
He'd found another sucker—had some fun.
But, silent, in her womb there grew a foal.
And he was born and named "Damask Of Gold".
He's still too young to prove what he might be.
I hope he carries on her legacy.
From lowly blood she came—to lowly bred.
But, on the racetrack *her* foals *could* turn heads,
As…on they raced and won…then, won some *more*.
I wish that she'd been *mine* those days of yore.
Fate dealt me poorer cards, yet…still…I played.
So, it was…I…who saw her waning days.
And it was…I…who fought to keep her young.
And it was…I…whose hope was never done.
Through years of trying…vet bills…surgery,
She did her best to give another *foal* to me.
But she had given far too much *before*.
There came a thunderous knocking on heaven's door.
For Death asked her to dance, as Death will do,
And, while dancing, took her foal, then took her too.
"Dollar A Dance", why did this have to be?
Why *couldn't* the *last dance* have been with *me?*

A Poem For Desert Whirlwind—My "Snoopy"

Most facets of society have guarantees.
That does *not* apply to *Racing*—just ask *me.*
The rule in Horseracing is "Buyer-Owner...Beware",
Or you'll get caught by lies or in Nature's snare.
I bought a beautiful mare three *years* ago.
I bought her at a fine, prestigious sale.
I paid four thousand dollars, plus the tax.
The star upon her forehead *should* have been an *axe!*
Sometime *before,* the axe had begun to fall.
Its weight lay on her withers like a *cross.*
It was a cross she carried to her grave,
For, though so many tried, no one could save.
They'd said she had an abscess—nothing more.
But, hidden 'neath the tape 'twas not *revealed*
That she had foundered quite some time before.
Once foundered *badly*—a horse lies at Death's door.
I turned her out on peaceful, pastoral hills.
The new-grown grass was lush and brilliant green.
These hills seemed like the hills of Paradise.
We did not know they were the Gates of Hell....
We could not see that they were *up in flame.*
For three long years, the flames licked at our souls.
Our mare was strong and brave, and of such good heart.
Each moment of her life was filled with pain.
She never breathed an easy breath *again.*
The rotated bones—like *nails*—drove through her hooves.
To turn, she had to *twist* on her back legs.
And if she walked at all, it was not far,
Although we fitted her with special shoes.
She never let the pain *color* her being.
She never let it turn her mean and sour.
All those who tried to help her *fell in love.*
The shoers and the vets did all that was in their power.

And, even in this most disabled state,
She was the *boss* in pasture, dell or barn.
The other horses all *deferred* to her.
She ruled them from her class, with strength and calm.
As years passed by, the bones turned more and more—
So much like *nails*—ever driving through her hooves.
She was so *loved*, I could not let her go,
Though life, for her, became a dreadful chore.
One last attempt—the doctor cut the nerve
So she could live…at last…without the pain.
She pranced and danced as she must have in days of yore.
Alas…it was to last a *day*—no more.
The surgery had cut off the blood supply,
So, as she pranced, her hoof began to die.
We guessed it was *the end*. The doc said, "No".
But he was *wrong*…. The time had come to go.
I wanted her to wait 'til I was there,
But Lori said she was in *great despair*.
We could not wait a day, or even an hour.
Death pressed down upon the cross with all His power.
They took her to the hill where breezes blow—
The hill that's taken precious lives before.
She was *so glad* that Death had come for her.
She stood…so bravely…calmly *awaiting* Him.
The specter drug had scarce coursed in her veins
Ere both her knees *gave way* and hit the ground.
Her *last breath* sounded almost like a *sigh*.
It seemed she knew the years of pain were done….

The little girl who lives there is not sad.
Her *heart* tells her this story has *no end*…,
And that Desert Whirlwind's running in the sky.
It whispers to her that "Snoopy", now, can *fly*.
And, so, she waits for "Snoopy" to come *back*
As one of our foals to be born next year.
She's sure we'll know which one is really "Snoopy".
And that's the one we'll hold *especially dear*.

Epilogue

The foal in her womb died with her….
Perhaps he was to have been my Champion….
His *mother* surely *was*….

Such Questions In My Soul Now Rage… When Mother's Womb Becomes A Grave….

A Poem For Pirate's Best And Her Foal

I had just worked two jobs.
I got home *past midnight.*
Then, I called *Lori*…my *mare was due* that night.
She said my mare was in "the foaling place".
I grabbed the carrots, got in my car…
And, so, began the race….
It was a race that we were all to lose.
We did not know it *then*…. It *seemed* good news.
Down at the bottom of a long hill was a small point of light.
I hurried down, so unaware of what waited in the night.
It was Death disguised as Life that waited there…
To catch a soul—*unborn*—within His snare.
Lori was worried. Things weren't going right.
The mare would push, and then, give up the fight.
She began delivering the *placenta* without the *foal.*
We watched some moments longer,
Then shivered—but not from *cold.*
And, so it was, we called the doctor in.
He, too, came down the hill—nearly at a run.
He looked at her and knew what must be done.
He reached *inside* her—tried to grasp the foal.
He could not figure out just how it lay.
He tried to *pull* but it was turned *askew.*
He did his best to figure out just how and what to do.
The time dragged on, and nothing could be done.
We hitched the trailer, loaded the mare,
And then, we made our *run.*
The clinic was about two hours away.
We got there *before* brooding night gave way to gloomy day….
A welcome light spilled out from their big barn…
Three people, busy, putting things in place.

This race with Death—never an *easy* race.
All hope to save the foal, by now, was *gone,*
Except that *glimmer* that…sometimes…stays too long.
We had to save the momma, if we could.
The mare was strong. That made our chances good.
They placed her in an iron chute that had strong metal plates,
Both at the front and at the back—to keep her in her place.
The doctor reached *inside* her—*shoulder* deep,
And, feeling hocks, knew that this foal was *breech.*
The chains went 'round its ankles,
And *then*…four people *pulled*…while I stood,
Crying, at her head and softly spoke to her.
Her haunches *jammed* against the metal plate
As they pulled on her foal with all their weight.
The doc—by far the strongest—was *laid back*
As a sailor leans out over the ocean…when his sailboat tacks.
The pulling, twisting…pulling had no end.
The tiny hooves, in chains, would not give in.
Then *finally* this *eternity* was o'er….
A perfect foal lay…dead…upon the floor.
Its front legs seemed to curve over its head,
As if it had been trying to hide from Death….
But Death can see in dark—He knows no bounds.
And Death is able to walk in places
Where…usually…*Life*…is found.
The doc said, "It's a filly". Then he moved her aside.
I knelt beside her—stroked her neck…
Ah, she looked *so alive*…I half expected her to breathe,
Then plant her hooves and *rise!*
So *beautiful*, and, yet, so *still*…I opened her closed eyes.
Her eyes were *bright. They were not glazed.*
My breath caught in *surprise!*
And to my touch, her body still felt *warm.*
But that warmth was her dam's, and not her own.
It, oh so soon, began to fade away.
Illusions—*all*—that gave hope, then *betrayed*….

For eleven months, the womb had given Life—
Protected her from all and helped her grow.
It *nurtured* her, fulfilled her every need,
But did not *warn* her she was *turned around.*
Deprived of oxygen, she quietly died.
The womb that gave her Life became her grave….
She looked so *perfect.…* How could she be dead?
Not ever to draw *first* breath or see the light….
Amidst my tears *tormented thoughts* now *stray…*
To all the *bills* I'll be required to pay…
For the *"priv-i-lege"* of knowing my foal died…
*There…*in the womb…while I stood…*just outside.*

A Poem For Minersville Flyer And
His Friend, Dan

His momma had the heart to win, but not much pedigree.
She had a stride that covered ground. Her name was Coroly.
As soon as his hooves touched the ground—
All he wanted *was to run!*
With his momma chasing *after* him—he thought it was *great fun!*
Then Fate took him to Utah snows, and taught him Utah *ways.*
There, folks worked hard. Their hearts were pure.
That's where he spent his days….
A man named Dan taught him the things
A racehorse needs to know.
He taught him *courage,* and how to "mind",
And helped his yearling grow.
He grew into a strapping colt,
Then grew into his *name*—
Minersville Flyer—flying from behind—
Would try to collar *fame.*
Third in a Derby—well on his way—
And all our hopes were high.
We thought it was his time to win,
But…that day…he began to die.
Blood filled his lungs…and…then…*disease.*
The doctors did their best.
We brought him home to his Utah snows
And…there…laid him to rest.

Diana and her Charlie

A Song For "Charlie"

He was not a Skip Away, a Free House,
or a Silver Charm, but he *tried* just as *hard*…
and was *loved* just as *much*.…

His birth was unremarkable.
At first, he seemed the same.
But he could run just like the *wind,*
So *racing* was his game.
He got his name from Mom and Dad,
From Grandpa—speed and heart.
Armed with these gifts, Tanyosho Dawn
Should tear the world apart.
But no one told him that some *gifts*
Can *curse* as well as *bless.*
And no one told him hearts too *great*
Put *bodies* to the test.
As years passed by, he fought his fights,
And even won a few.
The battles all were long and hard,
With no chance to renew.
His body grew a-weary
From the running with his *might.*
He had to learn to run through pain,
For that became his plight.
He raced with *many* jockey silks.
He raced for *many* men.
He raced for what seemed many years,
Then he *came home* again.
He thought the time had come to rest.
He thought he'd waged his wars.
He thought the battles…now…were done,
But, still, we asked for more.
We did not *heed* his whisperings.
We could not feel his pain.

We tried to patch up all the wounds,
And asked him to run *again*.
He *could* have stopped, refused and sulked.
He *could* have told us, "No".
But he did not.... His great, good heart
Dealt him the final blow.
He ran on heart, and heart, *alone*.
His body just gave way.
His body could not match his heart.
We put him down today.
We had no choice—the battle lost—
His leg was all but gone.
He hobbled bravely to his death—
His heart was still that strong.
Until the end, his gracious soul
Shone from his clear, kind eyes.
He ate a carrot from my hand,
Then I told him *good-bye*.
I stood with him upon the hill,
Wind ruffling through his mane.
His body slumped.... The specter drug
Had ended all his pain.
I knelt beside him on the ground
Until his soul was gone.
I cried, for it was not to this...
Tanyosho Dawn was born.
We had such hope for *better* things,
But *dreams* confounded *sight*.
Our dreams gave hope where there was *none*,
And...lost...not ...won...the fight.
If I could do it all...again,
So *different* would it be....
Death—held at bay—my "Charlie-boy"
Would still be...here...with me.

But We Just Called Him "Tommy"

Named for a story I wish was never told—
He died…himself…when he was two years old.
He was *so tiny* the night that he was born,
He needed help to stand and nurse—
And a *blanket* to keep him warm.
And, so it was, we *nicknamed* him "Tom Thumb",
And, in this world, I'm sure there's been just one—
Just one like him—so tiny…yet…so brave.
And I will never forget the joy he gave.
Just like his mother…kind…down to the bone.
He had her *strength*, but his *mind* was all his *own*.
He was so tiny, no fence could hold him in.
He roamed the farm—thought Dalmatians were his *kin*.
He'd *sleep* with them, curled up upon the porch,
Or lie with them on grassy knolls, avoiding summer's scorch.
He made *friends* with an ancient horse named "Fred",
Who was so old, he *should* have *long* been dead.
Fred still was baby-faced, with youngish eyes.
Though years had turned his body old,
They'd made him very wise.
There was not a barn-mate who did not honor him.
They seemed to sense he was the *patriarch*.
His power flowed-out from some warm, secret place.
He quietly ruled the farm with strength and grace.
Then, of a sudden, Tommy came along.
A *new* light seemed to *flash* in old Fred's eyes.
Fred took the little colt under his wing,
And taught him things that only horses know.
They raced and kicked and bucked all 'round the place.
And Tommy's friendship made Fred young again.
They'd nuzzle one another from their pens.
They'd share the *carrots* I brought from time to time.

I loved him so…two others loved him more—
The little girl and her mommy, who cared for him.
He *grew* up with the child upon his back.
She'd just climb up and sit—safe—without tack.
In his short life, he conquered many ills.
Without complaint, *swallowed* Life's bitter pills.
The maladies would *sometimes* get him down,
And slow his antics—so like a mischievous clown's.
He never *did* grow *big*, but he grew *strong*.
When he turned two, those hormones came along.
They made him think he was "the cat's meow",
And *whispered* of the fertile *fields* to plow.
And so, we had to send him to the vet
To change the blossoming stallion back to our pet.
But…oh…such simple things *sometimes* deceive.
A house may seem so full of *Life*,
But *Death* lurks in its eaves.
The doctor faltered—searched long, but could not find
The testicle, well-hidden deep inside.
Our Tommy slumbered long and slumbered deep,
And, though, we'd promised to *awaken* him—
It was a promise that we could not keep.
His once strong heart first *slowed*, and then…it *failed*,
As on the Reaper's scythe it was impaled.
And so, a precious life just slipped away
As Death descended, and His great power held sway.
In dreams…Tommy *curled up*…once *more*…by the door.
This time it was the door to Death….
He *shuddered*…then breathed no more.

Country Light

A Poem For My Beloved Stallion

I almost didn't buy you "Country Light".
Some others thought I didn't have the right.
In truth, I had just as much right as they.
I made a desperate final bid
As the gavel came *down* that day.
You have more dapples than the heavens have stars.
You make the path seem *clear*—the way—*not far.*
You make the suffering less—you ease the pain.
So many years of sorrow and death…
Perhaps, were not in vain.
I see a light when I look in your eyes—
A light that radiates and holds me fast.
It hypnotizes—makes me still *believe,*
Just when I thought the time for hope had passed.
I've been defeated in these *racing wars.*
But now a Champion's standing at my side—
His nostrils *flaring,* as he paws the ground,
His muscles *rippling,* as his great heart pounds.
My Champion is you, my Country Light.
Perhaps, together, we can find our way.
I dream that someday you will sire a foal
Who'll *catch the wind* and turn the *straw* to *gold.*
A foolish dreamer—*silly dream*—perhaps…,
But twists of Fate can lay the wildest things
In all our laps.
These twists of Fate can *give* or *take away,*
For twists of Fate deal dark of night,
But…also…light of day.
I hope you know I love you Country Light.
You are the ray of hope that's come
To lighten my dark nights.
Astride your back,

Hands tangled in your mane....
My cheek against your neck—
My lips will whisper of your fame.
Then we will ride into the mists of dreams,
As Fortune writes your legend on the winds.

Epilogue

I guess we will not ride into the mist of dreams together...
For he has gone before me.
Country Light, the nineteen-year-old stakes-winning son of
Majestic Light, and sire of a Champion, was humanely destroyed
on March 11, 2002. His owner and the ranch spent the last of
their assets trying to save this kind and beautiful stallion
whom they had grown to love. Country Light is buried in
a place of honor on the ranch where he was so beloved....

Red Earth

His name was dark and ominous.
We did not know it, then.
"Red Earth" *calls up* rich, living things—
Gold fields of ripening grain.
He grew so strong, handsome and fine—
His gleaming coat *aflame*—
A *fireball* of speed and heart—
A *tribute* to his name.
It was his *heart*, beating with *will*
And power…in his chest,
That spurred his body on and on
To *always* give its best.
And so, he loved to race in front,
And dared the rest to pass.
He tried so hard each time he raced…
And even to the last.
Flying in front, they *challenged* him.
His heart would not give way.
His body crumpled 'neath the strain.
We put him down today.
A body so willing…a heart—too strong,
A leg that snapped in two.
The Earth turned red with gallant blood,
And nothing more to do.
He'd pranced and danced in post parade—
Bowed neck and tossing head.
It's still too hard to, yet, *believe* my Champion is dead.

Death in the Afternoon…. A Tribute to Spook Express

And A Poem For Tom Skiffington, Robert
And Janice Aron, Andrea DeLong, Alcibiados
Polanco, and All Who Loved Her

A Festival…and then, some rain—
Not such a great surprise.
But this time heaven's trillion tears
Destroyed our greatest prize.
She hailed from far South Africa.
She ran with all her heart.
She brought us joy and pride and wealth—
Gave her all in every start.
But Fate will give, and Fate will take—
No *reason* to her rhyme.
The sun will shine…the clouds will roll…
As we *step up* to the line.
The clouds rolled in.
The rains poured down.
She waited at the gate.
Then our *beloved* Spook Express
Broke fast to meet her fate.
The sodden turf, drenched by the rain,
Torn up by flying hooves…
Made this a *dangerous* game to play.
Be we *heroes*, or be we *fools?*
She saw the wire—just…*there*…beyond….
She stretched with all her might.
But Fate stepped in and blocked her path,
And turned the day to night.
And…now…no winners *accolades*,
No saddle draped with flowers.
Instead…a body in repose
Which had given to its last hour.

The scene of her death—the shattered bones—
Symbols of shattered hearts—
Will *ever* burn in our memory
Of that day *dreams* came apart.

Death's Pale Flag

A Poem For Blushing KD And Those Who Loved Her

We watched, so sadly,
Death's pale flag *advancing*.
No words…no deeds
Could change or halt its course.
The breeze made *mischief*—
Catching up its corners,
Unfurling it above
Death's great black horse….
KD was born a chestnut ball of fire.
As Fate saw fit—she soon belonged to us.
She grew from frisky filly to a Champion—
Her heart so great that she could beat "the boys".
She ran for us and won almost a million.
She stole our hearts—became our greatest joy.
And…then…one *bad step* ended all the glory—
Made her Fate's puppet, and Death's favorite toy.
For three long years, she bravely took all comers.
With strength of will, she looked them in the eye.
Against each one she fought the gallant battle.
Her great heart beat, and would not let her die.
But even hearts like hers will finally tire.
And even *Champions* finally need to rest.
Though Death's pale flag has covered o'er her body,
Her legend *lives…truly…*she *was…*the best.

The Lion Roared...2001

A Tribute to Champions Who Have Lived,
And Some Who Will Never Be

Across the land a fitful breeze was blowing.
It *was* a breeze that *did not* bring relief.
It whispered of sad *things* it had been knowing—
Sad things it knew, but we had yet to see.
And March came in, as always, like a lion.
We could not help but hear its fearsome roar.
And it *seemed* "The Reaper" had some *scores* to settle—
Not enough *lives*...hungry...He came for *more*.
The winds of March were swirling all around Him—
Whipped at his cape—bent branches to the ground.
Yet, silently, He urged his black steed onward.
Nor did he ever lay His *dread scythe* down.
His gaze...alas...fell on the world of thoroughbreds—
The world of racing's best, who give their all.
It seemed those were the only ones he *wanted*.
And, one by one, they fell beneath his pall.
Weekend Surprise, Dahlia, and Charming Lassie,
Young Banshee Breeze, Con Game and Ryafan—
Some--old and feeble, some—just new-made mothers—
Gone...Champions all...no finer in the land.
Perhaps these winds of March, that blew through April,
Will finally lose their power, and then die down.
And Death will ride away—no longer hungry—
And leave us to lay our Champions in the ground....
But Death did *not* ride away.... He *stayed*...
And took more than two thousand of our babies.
Kentucky, we weep for you....
And we *salute* you....

Epilogue

The phrase "He stayed…and took more than two thousand of our babies" refers to the Mare Production Loss Syndrome (MRLS) which killed hundreds of close to term foals of 2001, and aborted thousands of the new lives forming in mares' wombs, which were to have been born the next year.…

The Last Sunset

A Poem For Seattle Slew And All Who Loved Him
February 15, 1974-May 7, 2002
Thank You Slew….

A *slew* of chances, a slew of dreams,
A *slew* of *many* things.
A *slew* is *much more* than "enough".
That's what he was, it seems.
A pact was made between girl and horse,
And sealed with just a glance.
A sale, a nudge, a nod, a bid…
And was it all by *chance?*
And he looked out upon the world
From *piercing* amber eyes.
He grew from gawky, gangly colt
Into its greatest prize.
Two girls, a logger, trainer, vet—
Caught up by thundering hooves—
Were *swept away,* as was the world,
As *he won* horseracing's *jewels.*
As yet to know the *sting of defeat,*
He won the Triple Crown.
This feat—unmatched in History—
Mixed magic with renown.
And then, some *tarnish* here and there
In this *imperfect* life.
But his courage shone for all to see—
Unblemished by the strife.
And "Slew" retired a Champion—
Became a Champion sire.
A girl, a logger, a groom, a horse
Shared a love that will ever inspire.
Though the *spirit* may well *dauntless* be,
The *flesh* grows old and tires,

As Father Time calls back the *spark*
He *gave* that lit the fire.
There…resting in the golden straw
With those who loved him best,
The setting sun lit amber eyes
Before they closed in death.

A Poem For Affirmed And
The People Who Loved Him

He had an *air* about him.
He *knew* more than his name.
He *toyed* with his opponents.
Each *race* brought him more fame.
Born of an *average* momma—
He was a Champion son.
He never was flamboyant,
But *knew* what must be done.
His eyes spoke of a knowledge
Beyond a horse's ken.
You'd watch him sizing up the scene,
Ignoring all the din.
He racked up nineteen *Stakes* wins.
He dueled great *Alydar*.
Most of the time, he beat him—
The distance—never far.
That's *what* made him so *special*...
He ran enough to win.
He seemed to know how much it took,
And that's what you got from him.
Fame laid its mantle on him,
And *glory* lit his way.
He walked its path so quietly...
He stole the show away.
No heady *overacting*,
No *temper tantrums* here.
He lived his life with kingly grace—
His *class*...by *all*...revered.
He was the last to win it—
The elusive Triple Crown.
Then thirty-seven *years* went by

Before American Pharoah
Took it down....
He *was a Champion* to the end.
It shone...there...in his eyes.
He'd always lived with *regal grace*—
With that same *grace*...he died.

No Laurels For Our Champion

A Poem For Exceller

Bred in America's "bluegrass" state
By Mrs. Charles *Engelhard*,
And sold to Nelson Bunker Hunt…
In *Europe* he made his start.
He was a "stayer", that's for *sure*—
A *closer* who could catch the wire—
With an *astounding* burst of speed,
And final *quarters* that *inspired*.
The only horse to ever *live*
Who, in the same amazing race—
Defeated two winners of the Triple Crown.
'Twas *he*…standing in the Winner's place.
Though *he* beat many *Champions*,
They never chose to honor *him*…
With the title of a "Champion".
That was the *first* of their sad sins.
Their *second* was…they let him *leave*.
To far-off Sweden he did go.
He hadn't done well *here* as a *sire*,
So…*far away*…came the final blow….
A *couple* crops on *Swedish* soil,
And then, some years lost to disease.
His owner—*bankrupt*—out of hope…
Ordered Exceller to be killed.
The body that had thrilled the world
Was *butchered* for its meat.
There…with his *blood*, his…*soul*…ebbed *away*
'Round his callous killer's feet….
His death inspired a *movement* here--
To save *the things* we've loved,
And to *give* our *horses*…the chance to *live*,
After *all* they've given *us*.

"I'm Saving This One For You"

A Poem For Ferdinand, Charlie, Shoe,
And All Our Lost Champions

The trainer—a *tall* man—horseman *extraordinaire*,
The jockey—a *small* man—with the strength of two—
Walked together to the big chestnut's stall,
Where, with a look that told he *"knew"*, the trainer turned
And *pointedly* said, "I'm saving *this* one for *you*...."
And so it was...a pact was *sealed*
Between the horse and two great men.
And so it was that Fate smiled down
On this brilliant chestnut, Ferdinand.
His eye was *kind*.... A *star* gleamed *out*
From a forehead, broad and wise.
His breeding did not have a flaw.
It shone...there...in his eyes.
He won the Derby—he and Shoe—
The last Shoe was to ride.
*Yes, h*e won the Derby—Charlie's *first,*
He *reigned* as Claiborne's *fine* grand prize.
He won the Classic, and Horse of the Year,
Three million *plus*, and grand *accolades.*
He retired at *five*, then tried to *pass on*
The "stuff" of which he was made.
But he could never *match himself,*
So, Claiborne passed him on
To the *Japanese*...across the sea.
His journey was *so long.*
And...there...he lived—the *gentlest* stud
His *new* groom *ever knew.*
And...there...he died—slaughtered for *meat*...,
And hardly left a clue.
We "found them out", but 'twas too late....
The deed had long been done.

His gentle spirit died with him
In the "house" where demons come.
With screams of horses all around,
Did *he* die *quietly?* I think he *did.*
That was his way.…
But it *does not comfort* me.
If the Japanese had made just one call
To America, across the sea,
A *thousand hands* would *have reached out,*
And not ever let this be.…
How is it that *our* great *Champion*—
Our grand, kind native son
Could ever walk the path to death,
Abandoned and unsung?
Some say, perhaps, we should *forgive,*
But I don't think I can.
And never will a day go by
Without tears for Ferdinand.
It's so *hard* to think "the stuff" of *Dreams,*
Of *Champions* and *Legends,* too,
Could end up *butchered* far from the love
That would have *saved,* if it only *knew.*…

"The Bid"

A Poem For Spectacular Bid

A striking *gray*…almost *black* in hue,
With power that did *abound*.
When he turned *two*, it seemed he could *run*…
Faster than any horse around.
Those old track records—he made them *fall*.
He was the reigning king.
He set the new ones track by track—
For all the world to see.
He bid for the elusive Triple Crown.
"Bud" Delp *thought* it was *won*.
But for a safety pin and a bad ride,
The deed would have been done.
He was America's *Champion*
For three years in a row—
Tenth of one hundred *great* racehorses
In one hundred years or so.
"Out of the money" just one time
In thirty grueling starts,
He posed "in the circle" twenty-six times.
His muscle matched his heart.
He went to stud for twenty-two *mil*—
A *record* at the time.
As years passed by with no *Champions*—
Hopes and dreams were on the decline.
His stud fee went from
One hundred and fifty thousand bucks
Down to three thousand five.
From Kentucky, they moved him to New York.
In 2003 he died.
He could not pass his *greatness* on….
And Fate *foiled* us again.
But the world still *waits* for the spark to *reignite*,
And give us… "The Bid" …again.

A Poem For Barbaro

The fairy tales of old were told to *teach*—
Teach little children not to go astray.
The endings, ofttimes, were very harsh and sad.
And so, The Ages exchanged *happy* for *sad*.
And so it was, "the woodsman" saved the day,
And Little Red Riding Hood did *not* get *eaten*.
And *true love's kiss* awakened fair Snow White.
And Hansel and Gretel outsmarted the old *witch*….
Then came the fairy tale of Barbaro…
That *foal* born in Kentucky's famous "blue".
That *foal* who grew into its favorite son—
Who, with his strength and heart, the Derby won.
The hopes of *many* rode upon his back
On the day the "second *jewel*" came around.
But *tragedy* struck that day instead of *joy*.
And he became Death's *pawn*—Fate's favorite toy.
Fate dangled him before a hopeful world.
New Bolton and Doc Richardson did their best.
The Jacksons spent the money, pulled all the stops.
For them and all who loved, there was no rest.
The horse was *gallant* in this fearsome fight.
But Nature built a creature who *can't survive*
An injury requiring *motionlessness*.
The laminae were compromised, then died.
And so… as Mother *Nature* dealt the cards,
The "racing world" finessed, and tried to "stay".
But *Nature* held a hand too *powerful*.
'Twas *Nature*, and not *Man* who won that day.
The day was late in January 0-Seven.
The *grim* news was delivered by his tearful vet.
Our *hero*, who had fought so *valiantly*,
Was gone forever—now, *forever* to be at rest.

We *know* that Mother Nature knows *not* of love—
Life lives or dies without Her smiles or tears.
Yet *Man* will *cherish* such as Barbaro,
And lay *upon* him *garlands*—well deserved.
The Ages could not change *this* story's end
As it changed the fairy tales in days of yore.
A horse is *strong*, but its *hooves* are—Oh-So-Weak.
And through this weakness, dark, dread Death can sneak.
We will long remember this great and gallant horse—
The horse whose battle enchanted *all the world.*
His ashes rest in Churchill's verdant green—
The place he showed the world what could have been....

The Ninth Bell

A Poem For Eight Belles

Eight Bells had *rung,* and all was well,
But, oh, what happened *then!*
It broke the back of racing's world—
The hearts of many men.
An owner, steeped in racing's wars—
A trainer who could *ride*—
A jockey, eager, fresh and young—
But none could turn the tide.
Eight Belles—born from the noblest lines—
Great heart that beat so *strong,*
Uncharted *Will* to give her *all*—
Such is the stuff of Song....
The bells rang out, and thousands *cheered!*
She'd beaten *eighteen boys!*
Then Fate stepped in, as *oft* She *does*—
We all become Her toys....
One ankle *went* when it should *not,*
The *other* could not last.
Fate brought this Champion to her knees—
Changed joy to breathless gasps....
Well raised, well kept, well taught, well *loved*....
But love can't always *save.*
The ninth bell rang.... Fate's callous hands
Dug—*deep*—our Champion's grave....

Rachel And The Boys

A Poem For Rachel Alexandra

The *girls* were just a passing thought,
So, *she* took on the *boys*.
Her greatness purchased for ten mil.
It caused a lot of "noise".
Some say she stole the Triple Crown
From 'cinderella'…"Mine".
But what is *precious* must be *earned*.
Is that *not* Life's *design?*
Some crowns—blood given, *some*—ill-gotten.
Some—won, *some*—undeserved.
This *legendary* Triple Crown,
Thrice difficult—thrice jeweled.
It has slipped through hands…
Fervent dreams—*destroyed*
By inches, furlongs—miles.
The *greats* still *great*,
But we must *wait*
For, yet, another while….

She trips the light *fantastic*
As to the post she goes.
She senses where the *wire* is.
That's where you'll find her nose.
Her thrilling charge from *last* to *first*
Makes *hearts* pound—*eyes* shed tears.
The world will ever *cherish* her—
Ever *love* her through the years.
She's mighty, mightae….

The Sixty-First Year

A Poem For J. C. Gonzalez

Sometimes a man is just a *boy.*
Sometimes a boy's a *man.*
The cards of Life fall randomly
As Fate deals out the hands.
She gathers *rosebuds*—gathers *thorns*—
She does not count the *worth*—
As She *takes back* the living souls
She chose to put on Earth.
She chose Juan Carlos—or was it *Joe?*
Not even *friends* were sure.
They only knew She'd dealt him cards
That he did not deserve.
No more industrious could he have been--
No heart of greater depth.
His loyalty was beyond reproach.
He stood for what was best.
But Fate saw fit to take the words
That he spoke to a friend,
"Beware this racetrack's *dangerous",*
And She *used* them against *him....*
A horse with hidden injuries
Was racing—giving all.
Sometimes the giving of *too much*
Precipitates the *fall.*
And, so it was, this quiet boy,
Whose virtues made a man,
Was taken in the midst of Life—
Cut down by Fate's cruel hand.
The legs that snapped—the thundering hooves—
The way that he was thrown
All added up to instant death,
As Fate crushed flesh and bones.

THIS death—the first in sixty-one years
Of "racing" at this track—
Silenced the crowd, who could not *see*
Why God must take him back.
The "show" did not go on that day—
It would have drowned in tears
For this inspiring jockey who met with *Death*
When the wire seemed so *near*.

When Demons Dance With Champions....

A Poem For Chris Antley...
January 6, 1966-December 2, 2000

When Demons dance with Champions, the Demons ofttimes *win*.
Like *sirens*—vixens *clothed* in night—they beckon them to *sin*.
With graceful arms and flowing hair,
And with such haunting voices—
The sirens call them to their doom—
Weave illusions that taint their choices.
And...so it was...a young man's dreams *came true*...
For *just a while,* as with his touch, his horses *won*.
Fate had blessed him with Her smile.
Friends say Chris *rode* with *special grace*—
That he could *feel* his horse....
As "one" they'd cross the wire on wings,
No matter what the course.
His prowess opened up the doors to glory, fame and gold.
But, unbeknownst, through these *same doors*...
Demons...in silence...stole.
He rode a Champion—saved his life—
But could not save his own.
The drugs and *Demons* conquered him.
He died...young and alone.
And...so it was...by *desperate choices*
His golden light was dimmed.
Yet, still, it shines in hearts that love,
As they *remember* him.

Laffit

A Poem For Laffit Pincay, Jr.

Too *big* to be a jockey.
Too *small* to play *baseball.*
Yet a *fire* burned *deep* in the heart
Of Rosario's little boy.
He travelled up from Panama.
He left his *good friends* there.
He faced a *new* and big, wide world
With *loneliness* to spare.
Fred Hooper and Cotton Tinsley
Helped put him on firm ground.
His *dedication* did the rest…
His *story* now renowned.
He rode for D. Wayne Lucas—
Made *friends* with tiny "Shoe".
He married Linda, whom he did so love.
To *himself* stayed ever *true.*
He won the Derby on star-crossed Swale,
Helped Affirmed out-duel "The Bid",
Rode Landaluce into history—
And still had time to love his kids.
He carried *Spend a Buck* across the wire…
Won *Breeder's* Cups…*Gold* Cups, too.
He *starved* himself for years on end
To make his dreams come true.
His *dedication* was *unmatched.*
The *fire* burned within.
His strength in legs, shoulders, and arms,
Ofttimes did *his* foes in….
Life took his wife *away* from him
In a most *tragic* way,
Then sent him a blue-eyed "breath of spring"
To help *keep* his *grief* at bay.

"The Shoe" had warned him that the"Big 5-0"
Is not a *pretty thing*.
The owners and trainers oft *bail out*,
And leave aging jockeys…*wondering*.
"Over the hill"—always *half-starved*—
He never gave up faith.
A wiry old lady with a bowl of fruit
Helped him stay in the race.
He rode the *slump* like a champion.
He made it go away.
He matched his *courage* with his *strength*,
As he *had* done *every* day.
This quiet man with Strength of Will
Has *shown* what can be done.
He *rode* the Champions—*beat* them, too,
During *his* "Time *In* The Sun".

The Tin Woodsman

A Poem For Gary Stute…My Friend

So long ago I met a boy—
Oh, how the passion burned!
And we were young, and it was fun—
A fine *tryst* for all concerned.
Then each of us went on with Life.
I'd see him here and there.
And, when I did, the laughter came—
A tonic for despair.
I did not know he'd judged *himself*
With *righteousness* unbending.
I did not know he'd plunged his soul
Into dark of night…unending.
He claimed that he'd been *ever* cruel,
When he had just been honest.
He claimed that he deserved his lot,
With *all* its terror and tarnish.
We do not get what we *deserve*
Here, on this *little* Earth.
We simply get just what we get—
No better…and no worse.…
Do not condemn yourself for things
You've made up in your mind.
It was *not for wrong* or errant ways
That Fate's been so unkind.
The Woodsman's wish was for a heart.
You think you need one, too.
You have one bigger than the sky.
Your life proves this is true.
Do not say you just *wait* for death,
Nor care for things of Earth.
Do *not* belittle what *you* know
Of *horses* and their worth.

You are just *human*—fallible—
Things we *all* do *may* seem *cruel*.
The *mirror* shows a different being.
Believe or be a fool!
You're sorry for breaking all those hearts,
But they broke just a *little*.
If *you* give up on *your* life *now*,
You'll split them down the middle.

Charlie, We Miss You

April 13, 1913-April 20, 1999

The search may last a *whole lifetime,*
Yet…still…it's hard to find
Much evidence of *redeeming traits*
In this species called "Mankind".
Then, of a sudden, comes a *being*
In the trappings of a man—
His goodness strengthened by his *class*—
His *name*—Charles Whittingham.
His heart e'er beat with boundless love.
His soul overflowed with grace.
He helped so *many* to find their way—
To *know* they had a place.
He *loved* his horses. He *knew* them well.
He *knew* just what they thought.
This mystic gift in trainer, renowned
Was *born*—could not be bought.
So great in stature, so great in love,
So great in grace and class—
Too fine a man to bully or brag,
Or *other's* faults to blast.
And, if you erred, he just forgave—
Stretched out a needed hand.
His voice and ire were never raised.
He was that kind of man.
And those who knew him were so blessed.
His greatness *lifted* them.
Our fondest *wish* for such as him
Is Life that has no end.
But, just as Life must breathe its *first,*
So Life must breathe its *last.*
The time—however *long*—too *short,*
The days too quickly *pass.*

Yet he will *e'er live* in our hearts—
His footprints *e'er* mark the sand.
His legend…*true*…will *e'er* live on—
Our *friend*—Charles Whittingham.

The Darkling Plain

A Poem For Eddie Gregson
August 7, 1938-June 5, 2000

His demons danced within his mind.
His horses crossed the wire.
His *soul* told him he must be *best*,
And *burned* him with that fire.
To those who loved him, he gave love.
To friends, he seemed so wise.
To those who knew him, he was fine.
His strength shone from his eyes.
A life—so varied and so full—
He'd done so *many* things....
Perfection always beckoned him,
And *made* him wear her ring.
But Life's *imperfect...*
So are we all...
Too much for him to bear.
His demons taunted, then they laughed—
And left him lying...there.

A Poem For Carole Beers.... 1935-1999

She called about an *ad* I ran
To sell "Prowling For Gold".
But he was not the horse for her.
This fact...to her I told.
We *both* liked dogs.
We *both* liked cats,
And **most** critters who draw breath.
The things we shared built a strong bond—
Our friendship true and best.
She entered "Racing" with a *flair*,
And *Luck* stood at her side.
She thought it was an *easy* game.
Her "Kristilar" was her pride.
We sought a piece of Paradise
In valleys deep and green.
Together, we picked *out* a spot—
No *fairer* could be seen.
We pooled our assets for the "down".
And then I helped her *move*.
Alas, I had to stay *behind*,
With too much left to do.
Children had I, and horses, too,
With *retirement* far away.
The bills—tremendous...money—scarce,
So...I...worked every day.
She tried to share her *luck* with me,
But...*too soon*...it was gone.
It left us both with little hope—
And, oh, the days were *long*.
I saw *the green hills* through her eyes,
For I could never *come*.
The wolf was always at my door,

And I was on the run.
Her mares broke down.
Her colt got sick….
The money just ran out.
She counted friends on *just one hand*—
The rest she held in doubt.
We kept in touch by notes and phone,
And *shared* our separate plights.
The "Racing World" had *barred* its teeth,
And we'd lost all the fights.
But her *last* fight I knew not of.
She fought cancer *courageously.*
Calm, steady Marcy cared for her,
And kept her company.
She left this earth 'midst our green hills.
She quietly slipped away.
I had *wondered* why she hadn't *called….*
The *answer* came today….

Crusty Ole Wisdom

A Poem For Bob Swartz (BS)

I ran a *horse* ad…met a man—
Though only on the phone.
But he became a *special* friend,
Just from his words, alone.
He seems to *understand* the thoughts
Behind the things I say.
His grasp of Life—*remarkable*—
As he's lived it…full…each day.
He has no fear of what people *think*
Because he knows who he is.
His words can help me to *accept*
Sad things that shouldn't be.
He *realizes* Life is God's great joke,
And the joke's on *all* of us.
He knows we must just *try* to *laugh*—
Try not to fret and fuss.
He likes his women—likes his booze.
He *loves* his family.
He *knows* that life is not all *that*
It *was cracked up* to be.
He may be crusty, brusque, and rough,
And…*tough*…on the outside.
But honor, wisdom, and a heart of gold
Are hidden…just inside.
Somehow…his voice makes me feel safe—
Makes me feel "it's all right".
He gives my soul a little rest
From this "*War*" that we call "*Life* "….
He's what you call a "*character*".
He's what I call a friend.
He's who you'd *want*…there…at your side
When Life comes to an end.

Jacquelyn And The Wild Blue

A Poem For Mike Ames And His Mom

Born way *back* in 1912
In a small Texas town.
There, as a *girl*, she was bored to *tears*,
With *no "action"* anywhere around.
And, so, her *big* bro taught her *well*
About how to "dust the crops".
And *she* became a "*flying ace*"—
FORGET dusters or mops.
And then she moved California way—
And *acted* for RKO,
Until *Warner Brothers* stole her *away.*
But she failed to steal the show.
Then on she went to Cloverfield To hone her pilot skills.
Her skills were, now, in great demand,
As Nazi *evil* spread 'cross the world.
America, not yet in the war—
Still *helped* as best it could.
It gave its old friend, England--
Fuel, *bombers*, supplies, and goods.
America bid Jacquelyn
To take the *bombers* there—
To England's lush and verdant fields
That, *now*, had been laid *bare.*
The German missiles, bombs, and strafe—
The German power and terror
Had changed the face of *all the world,*
And left it in despair.
She flew the bombers—faced the fear.
With her *prowess* she set them down—
Faced power wires, just missed the trees—
Carved out a name…renowned.
She and another Jacqueline—

Fast friends, and pilots…true—
Were so important to the cause,
America paid them their *due*.
Just "five feet two" and, yet, she stood
As *tall* as any man.
She bumped a *colonel* off a *transport* plane.
And *that* sure made him *mad*!
She fell in love on English shores—
An RAF pilot she wed.
And, in her womb, a *life* now bloomed
That *changed* the things she did.
"My *dad* was killed before I was born,
So, it was just *mom* and I."
We had a *quiet* life, *filled* with love—
She'd *already* made *history*.
The *mystery* of parents' genes
Gave me some brains and heart.
They also gave the gift of seeing
Some *humor* through this "dark".
She loved horse racing. I *learned* her love.
Together, we would drive to Santa Anita—our favorite track.
It was good to be alive!
Mom taught me lessons *tenderly*—
Oft with her tongue-in-cheek.
I learned from her and I loved her well….
Que sera sera…so it was and it will *be*….
Now *she's* been gone these *many* years,
Yet…still…she lives with me.
I'll ever honor who she was,
And who she is to me….

Don And Jean

A Poem For My Friends, The Engels

Don and Jean Engel—so *much* like Roy and Dale—
Lived in a love that inspired…strength and grace dallied there.
They practiced *virtues*, nurtured *values* that *are* so seldom *found*….
Made a home *full of warmth,* where kind *love* did abound.
And their family blossomed as the love showered down.
Their goodness came easy.
Their advice—always sound.
He created a "letter" that challenged Racing's *misdeeds*,
Gave advice, brought a chuckle, lent a thought—sowed a seed.
I *count* myself *lucky* that my path crossed with *theirs*.
When I heard their kind voices, it would ease my despair.
And their love for each other is a legend, for sure,
For I know that no other was so strong and so pure….

Magic in his hands…*wonder* in their hearts—
These two look out *upon* the world
With *understanding* and "a touch of class",
And flags of gentility…*unfurled.*
He can paint "the horse"—reach into his soul.
He can paint the souls of men.
He can paint the *brilliance.*
He can paint the *strength.*
He can make them *live* again.
And he chose a *soul mate,* oh so long ago
Who's stood…always…there—at his side.
She has been his partner—she has been his love
Ever since she was his bride.
I am ever honored to have known these two,
And for them to call me "friend".
They have given *beauty* to a struggling world
With their hearts, *brushes,* and pens.

Lori

A Poem For My Special Friend, Who Loved And
Cared For My Horses For All These Many Years

Through twists and turns of *happenstance,*
I met a future friend—
So capable, so full of Life,
So pretty, lithe…so thin.
Most *women* did not care for her.
Her beauty *angered* them.
To me she was a breath *so pure,*
She invited *sunshine* in.
And *Indian* blood coursed in her veins—
Her spirit—tall and proud.
A mane of blonde, and deep-set eyes—
She *stood out* in a crowd.
She was a *horsewoman*—extraordinaire.
She *loved* birds, cats, and dogs.
She raised two girls with strongest steel—
Tempered with fun and love.
As a young girl—oh, she could *ride!*
The horses jumped for her.
Lady *Godiva*…on a horse,
With clothes and boots and spurs.
She rode a horse for Jerry Buss.
"Twas he who took the fall.
Her beauty just *enchanted* him.
You can't blame him, at all.
But a gilded cage was not for her.
And so, she said "good-bye".
She dealt …from the top.
Slung from the hip,
And *seldom* did she lie.
When…I…met her, she managed Ralphs….
What *stories* she could tell

Of *shoplifters*, of dumb, dumber, *dumbest*,
Of *comedy*, of *hell*....
A haughty girl came in, one day
With a *bagful* of "returns".
I'm *hoping* that what happened *next*
Will be a lesson to be *learned*.
Lori leaned over…glanced in the bag,
Asked, "Do you think I'm *dumb?*
That's not *Ralphs'* stuff, so take it *back*
To where you *stole* it from".
For many *years* my horses stayed
With her…there…amidst her hills.
Her girls would dangle 'round the broodmares, necks—
Climb up on their pipe corrals.
Of tragedies, of hopes, of dreams,
Of death, of Life, and more—
My broodmares brought forth "little ones",
But failure hid behind the door.
Fate drained me of my hope and will.
My money, now, all gone.
Lori and I took different paths….
Her "ex" took back the farm.
She met a man who was a "man",
Yet quaked beneath her gaze.
They made a match.
They made a pact,
And headed *Idaho* way.
She found a house all filled with light
Built on *wide, lush* fields of green.
And—there--she lives with those she loves—
Her love of Life still keen.
There, with her girls, her humor—strength,
And with her gallant *white* horse, Dude—
There, with her husband, her "minnies", dogs…
She coaxes from Life…all…that it will give.

Truckin' On Down The Road

A Poem For Sandy And Lee And San Lee Ranch.

Her childhood days were pretty tough.
Her mother couldn't "love".
Her *dad's* folks hailed from *Switzerland*,
With its snowy *mountains* towering above.
They settled in the bluegrass state—
Built a business making *jam.*
Her father loved her mother,
Who…alas…did not *give* a damn!
They had a boy, then parted ways.
To California her dad would go
She chose to stay, but couldn't cope, alone,
With the cold Kentucky snows.
So, he *brought* her to the sea and sun—
He thought it would warm her soul.
Then, whoops, they had another child—
But her heart remained ice-cold.
Their little girl was tough as nails.
She really had to be.
Surviving a mom who *could not love*
Is no *small task,* you see.
She left *home*…set out on her own…
When she was seventeen.
She learned to ride. She learned to "truck"—
Not afraid of *anything*!
She met a man, born in the South.
He had a *"cowboy"* past.
It happened he was *fearless*, too,
And, so, the die was cast.
He trained his tigers. She rode her broncs.
They *both* knew how to *"truck"*.
They crossed this land from sea to sea…
Pulled each *other* from the muck.

They met so *many* characters.
They faced so *many* trials.
The memories, though not always *good*,
Were…*mostly*…always *wild*.
They settled down, and built a ranch
Just on earth's outer edge.
And there, they lived outside the grid,
With horses, dogs, and cats.
Their peacocks call.
Their chickens lay.
The broodmares deliver their foals.
They spend their days breeding their fine stud—
A "Champion" is their goal.
I *hope* they reach their goal someday.
They'll share it all with me.
I "hold the gates". They do the work—
My friends, Sandy and Lee….

When Death Waits At The Wire…

A Poem For Trainer Clare Juarez, Her Jockey
Amando, And The Horses That They Loved

Against all odds—and then some—
That's how they lived their lives.
They fell in love—the jockey
Took the trainer for his wife.
And *then*, they raised two colts
Who had same *dam*, but different *sires*.
And *each* raced at his level—well.
And *each* was full of fire.
The jockey took the colts up north
To enter in a race.
A four-horse trailer carried them,
With a *screen* that had no place.
Because the colts were such good friends,
He thought it would be *safe*…
To put the screen between the two,
And tie it in its place.
But when he gave them each their grain,
The two began to spat.
The screen became a *deadly* thing
That ripped one horse apart.
Amando *tried* but could not *save*…
And so gave up the fight
A life so precious to them both
Was ended there that night.
In memory of this horse they loved,
They bought another foal
Whose sire was just the *same* as *his*—
Whose story now unfolds….
When he grew up, *he* was so *fast*,
Officials claimed they lied.
So…more than once he was *turned down*

When he had qualified.
The time dragged on, and still no race.
The end of patience neared.
Amando learned that *cancer* reigned,
And it was worse than *feared*.
A mighty *struggle* did ensue
Between Death and the man.
Determined, still, to ride his colt,
He *would not* take Death's hand.
And…so…Death waited at the wire—
Their young colt drew the *rail*.
The trainer *begged* them *not* to run,
But her jockey's wish prevailed.
Three lengths in front—running *full-out*.
The colt stepped in a hole.
This rail had swallowed too many a *horse,*
If *truth* were to be told.
He *dragged* himself across the wire
On *three* legs and his heart.
He looked into the eyes of Death,
And light gave way to dark.
The jockey knew it was his last ride—
His last heroic act,
For with his colt, his
Will was *lost*
That day upon the track.
His *cancer grew…*
Clare nurtured him, But it was all in vain,
As cancer spread like *wildfire,*
And laid him low with pain.
The day he drifted into death,
The *reins* slipped from his hands.
She *reached* to catch them, but…*alas…*
They slipped like grains of sand….
Horse racing deals is flesh and blood.
Most *horsemen* deal in *love.*

They know not what waits at the wire—
Decreed from up above.
They *try so hard.*
Their days are *long.*
And their *rewards* are *few.*
But *horses* gallop in their dreams,
And give them strength, *anew.*
It's hard to *understand* this breed—
Consumed by urgent quest
To raise and run a "Champion"—
To give the world "the best".
There's *suffering* here, but *real love,* too—
Though *tears* oft douse its *fire.*
For *greatness* always has *great* costs…
And Death waits at the wire.…

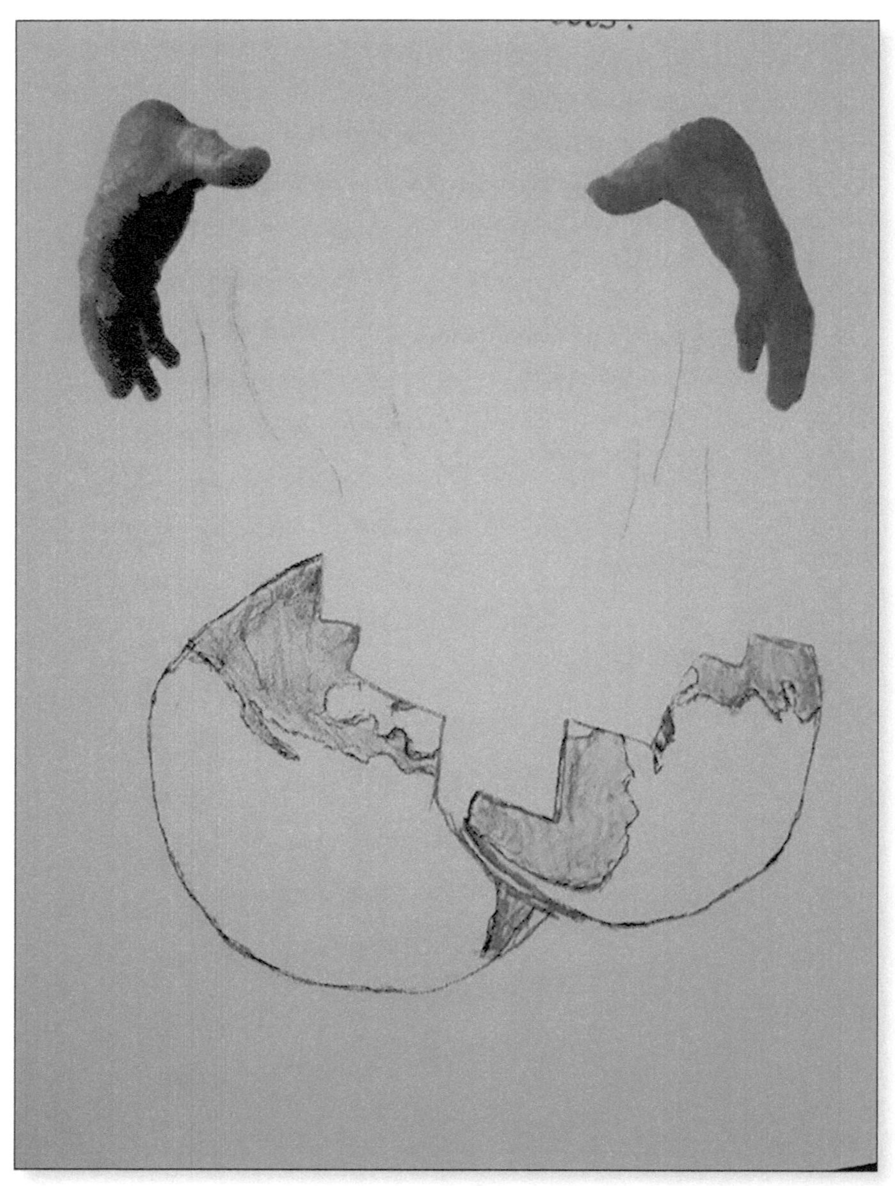

He's Got The Whole World In His Hands?

Flight 261 Has Landed

Those eighty-eight—handpicked by God
To go to that "better place"—
To *worship* him upon their knees—
To *wonder* at his grace.
They join the trillion wispy souls
Applauding a *jealous* God.
They *dare not* glance to right or left.
They *dare not* doubt his Word.
Their worship—never *interrupted*—
For there's nothing else to do.
Eternity stretches *endlessly*
For these *trillion "chosen few"*.
The *evidence* that they ever *lived*
Now rests *entirely*
In the hearts and minds of those left behind—
Or things *floating* in the sea.
And what of those now left behind?
Are they supposed to be…
Overwhelmed with *joy* at whom God *chose*
To perish in the sea?
Their *pain*—far too much to endure.
Their *loss*—too much to bear.
So, they *cling* to the thought of *Paradise,*
With their loved ones waiting there.
And so it is that Heaven *lives.*
We *need* it…so…to be.
Without it we'd lose all we love
For…all…*eternity.*
And so, the hope of *something more*
Helps loosen our despair.
It's just *too hard* to live and die
Without *souls* or *trumpets' blare*….

The Tragic Tale Of Egypt Air...Flight 990

A little boy of *four*
Said, "Please don't go"!
But he was just a *child*,
And so, they *went*.
So full of hopes or dreams or plans...,
They came—
Exchanged their boarding passes
For watery graves.
There was one amongst them
Who was filled with great *despair*.
It was in his *fearsome* hands...rested their fates.
Their hopes and dreams
And plans and lives—*snuffed out*
By one lone man—
The Devil's advocate.
So evil—perhaps it was SATAN...*Himself*...
Who sat with him, and
Helped him pray to God.
And...while God *slumbered*,
This man *dallied* with Fate—
Seduced Her with his *false, hypnotic* words.
And...while God *slumbered*,
Who listened—*TELL ME*—Who?
Just careless Fate,
Who had *twisted* this man's *soul*....
Just cunning Fate,
Who had *blessed* them all by day...
Then...in dead of night...
Took all the blessings...*away*.
And thus it was, a lone man in despair—
Overwhelmed...and set on taking his own life...
Was just too weak or bitter to die *alone*,

And so took two hundred and sixteen other lives.
So *many* murdered by this *single* man….
Why couldn't God give "Good" the upper hand?
Why couldn't the plane's true pilot win the fight
For the *controls* as the plane dived through the night?
A Demon placed his soul in God's own hands
By speaking a prayer that is a *mockery*.
For…if there were a God who really cared,
Why would so many have lost their lives
In that cold, forbidding sea?
Now that the plane has *dived*, the lawsuits *fly*.
But they hardly ever sue the guilty ones.
Instead…they go to where the money is,
For what good would suing Fate or God
Do *anyone?*
An airline cannot stop the hand of God,
For God is *Great*, and *He has so much power*.
An airline cannot find *insanity*
When it only *shows* itself in that final *hour*.

We Did All That You Asked...

A Poem For Christine

A little girl—the last of *eight*
From Cath-o-lics...*devout*,
Who are told, "Go out and *procreate*!"
They did the things that they were told—
Worshipped so piously.
They gave the *money*—gave the *time*....
Salvation's never free.
But...why...if what they were told is true...
Should God look down, one day,
To see their child of just fourteen...
An...then...whisk her away?
A cheerleader—a friend to all,
A spirit—wholesome—a face...so fair,
Was jogging on a dead-end road—
Safe—since it led nowhere.
Yet, Death, in guise of a wedding guest,
Chose just this place to drive.
His fingers gripped the steering wheel,
As he peered through bloodshot eyes.
Too weary from the toils of Life—
Or from too much champagne,
The eyelids closed, the fingers relaxed....
But...where...to lay the blame?
As sleep overcame the wedding guest,
The dominos began to fall—
A curb, a pole, and then...a child—
The four wheels hit them all.
Her family, sitting by her bed,
As she lost her grip on Life,
Must surely have wondered
Why God's Pure Love
Would ask such sacrifice....

Where Has Our Polly Gone?

A Poem For Polly Klaus

Her name was *Polly*.
She was twelve years old…
A child fair of face and sweet in soul.
Her giggling friends were *gathered* in her room—
To laugh and talk 'til dawn, then *sleep* 'til noon.
The bedroom door was *shut* to keep the *merriment* inside.
Alas, no one gave even a thought to the window—opened wide!
'Twas through this window, cloaked in silence,
Crept a *twisted* FIEND.
The giggles faded at the sight,
And…yet…there were no screams.
He used their *fright* to seal their *lips*,
As he snatched up his prey,
Then *disappeared* into a night
That *never* turned to *day*.
She *never* saw the sun again—
Blue sky, or grass that's green.
The smile that once lit up her face
Was *nevermore* to be seen.
He used her youth and *bloom*
To try to prove he was a man.
Instead…he proved that evil can
Crush good with just one hand.
But where was
God on this unholy night?
Was He fishing, hiking, or watching a good fight?
Was He biking, golfing, or shopping at the mall?
Was He playing cards, croquet or *basketball*?
I do not know the *answers* to all this.
Such a death casts my belief into the abyss.
For what *great power* of GOOD could so *ordain*
That *innocence* be lost in death and pain?

What father—born of Heaven or Earth—
Had he *the power to SAVE*—
Would let his child face terror alone,
Then lay her in the grave?
The *Earthly* father had *NOT* the power to save.
The *Heavenly* father just chose to *look away.*
So on this vile and fearsome night
Her lifeblood ebbed away.
Were you to ask just where it went,
I could not truly say….
I can say THIS…
If it were up to me…,
Such things as this
Would never…ever…be….

Her smiling eyes won't *see* again.
Her new *teeth* won't grow in.
Her precious soul has left this world.
So has her sparkly grin.
How can this *happen*? How can it be?
I do not *understand*....
How *could* a fiend of *such* magnitude
Have *walked* here as a man?
Could *no one see something* was *wrong*,
Or feel the evil there?
Did his mother, siblings, lovers, friends
Not know...or just...not care?
And as this twisted being grew up,
So did his sick desires.
His fancy turned to tiny girls.
His own child burned in his fires.
Our *hallowed* "Justice" truly *was* blind.
She set this monster free...
Even after he'd exposed his evil soul—
And *whispered of what* was to be....
Samantha sat upon a wall,
Laughing—*playing* with her friend,
Without a thought of what would be
Or that her life would end.
"This Evil" saw her sitting there,
And turned his car around.
He snatched her up, and disappeared
Before an *alarm* could sound.
Her *gramma* heard and called for help.
Her *mother* fell apart.
The *world* had *hope*, and prayed to *God*,
And tried to sort things out....
They found her body, tossed on a *hillside*—a tiny life *snuffed out*.
The next time that you pray to God, ask how this came about....
Sort as you *may*.... Search as you *might*....

There's no way to explain
The *reasons* that this little girl should *die* in such great pain.
Where was the "LOVE"
The night he took this precious little girl—
Made her endure *terror* and *pain*
Before she left this world?
How could he have lived for all these years,
And not have given signs
That he was spawned in depths of hell,
And *ruled* by damaged mind?
As Life goes on, and pages turn,
I laugh less than I cry.
I ponder things beyond my ken,
And seek *answers* for the *whys*….
Man seems so *foolish*—so *naïve*—
Works to win a game or prize,
Then…*doesn't* thank *the ones who helped*…
Instead…praises the *skies*.
I can't find answers anymore.
I'll give up, by and by.
For…what God would help *win a football game,*
Then *let Samantha die?*

The Lost Children Of Ireland

As *God* sits on his *throne*, above all *blame*,
His "Faithful" rant and rave and *praise* his name.
But who *gives* a "*rat's ass*" HOW Mankind *worships* a God
That he *created* from his own
Insecurity and Wonderment?
And even if you care a little...HOW...
Is it worth the lives of three young boys, who
Burned in the fires of Hell...here...on this Earth?
Is it worth the lives of *twenty-eight*...
Blown to tiny bits...IN HIS NAME...
And IN HIS MERCY?
Man has suffered *mightily* in the name of God....
God said, "I am a *Jealous* God".
Might I *also* add "*Egotistical* and Cruel"?
Perhaps man's creative process went awry
The day he made this *GOD* of his....

The Bargain....

The Story Of The Twin Towers, The Pentagon,
And The Grassy Field—Thousands Of Lives...
Exchanged For ONE God's Smile....

Their God *rejoices....*
Ours...is somewhere...*hiding.*
And...still...we worship Him and call His name.
Were he a man...on "Row of Death" now biding,
With *lawsuits* by the *thousands*...for the pain.
What's in a God?
It's just what men have put there.
OURS is an egomaniac without power.
It seems to me He also lacks *compassion.*
Yet...still...we call Him in our darkest hour.
It was men of *Faith* who thought *their* God had *bid* them
To give their lives to bring the Towers down.
And has their God now taken them to heaven?
Or do their tortured souls burn 'neath the ground?
AMERICA turns to its God for solace....
Where was its God the day the die was cast—
At Logan, Dulles, Newark or Manhattan,
Or our "Seat of Power" or the field of grass?
I think He must have been at other venues,
And had some *pressing issues* on his mind.
How *else* can you explain His total *absence*
The day *thousands* of people lost their lives?
In His own words... translated from the Bible,
He tells us that He IS a "jealous" God.
He tells us we cannot partake of VENGEANCE,
For "VENGEANCE is all Mine", sayeth the Lord.
Amazing! He *admits* to all those *vices!*
He's *jealous,* vengeful and above the law.
When things go *RIGHT,* we are taught to give Him *credit.*
When things go *WRONG,* it's because Mankind is *flawed.*

And when we've waded *through* Life's pain and suffering,
And our bodies die—shades of what they used to be—
Our *great reward* is to *worship* him…forever—
Heads bowed, in reverence, o'er our bended knees….

234

PART II

WISDOM FROM THE HAIKU

From The Profound to the Profane

The price that we must
Pay for "Life" is "Death".…. Always
Has been and *will* be.

About the time you've
Figured it all out…things *change*…
Then they change, again.

He opened a can
Of worms and…*then*…he wanted
To close it.…. TOO LATE!

I've got a lot of
Irons in the fire!!! BUT…
The fire *went out!!!*

Each of us was…once…
Someone's child. Some were *loved,* some…
Not. Then "Life" happened.

Once…someone rocked us.
Alas…not *anymore,* for
Now…we have grown up.

It is sad to have
To Pay The Fiddler when you
Don't really *owe* Him.

Whoever wrote, "Some
Days are Diamonds, Some Days are
Stones" *knew* about *Life.*

Hopes and Dreams can help
Us go on, even if they
Never *DO* come true.

When we get tired of
Following our *Elusive*
Dreams…*darkness* may come.

"Duh" *words of wisdom*
ABOUND, and some of them aren't
Even *true* or *wise.*

Whoever thinks, "What
Goes around *Comes* around" has
Not BEEN *around* long.

"Causes"…slippery
Slopes that *change,* and *"bob and weave"*—
Become something *else.*

There is more than ONE
"Waterloo" in a Lifetime….
Trust me on *that* one.

"The Wild Blue Yonder"—
EVER a fascinating
Notion to ponder.

So *strange* when you fly
HOME to Life that *was,* then BACK
To a Life that *is.…*

Driving freeways in
The Dead of Night…. Cars speeding
By with *all* those lives.

Those things we *choose* to
Believe can bring peace or angst
In this troubled world.

There are things I think
About that break my heart, and…
It will *always* be.

We are *alive* for
Just a *little,* but *many*
Things are wrought there-in.

NEVER say "never",
Except *just this ONCE,* because…
You just NEVER know.

If you let folks *"off*
The hook" for *wrongs,* it's hard to
Get them back on it.

Find a paddle FIRST,
And…*then*…head up "Shit Creek". It's
The only damned *way!!!*

A COMMENT ON "THE FICKLE FINGER OF *FATE*"
Fate's a *horny* Bitch.
She likes fucking…. Evidence
Is all *around* us!

There's "DRUNKENNESS" and
There's "The *Devil* may *care,* but
I…don't…DRUNKENNESS".

Some *talk* about things
They've never *done*…keep quiet
On things they *have* done.

From now on, all my
Friends are gonna *be strangers*….
No Expectations.

A COMMENT ON THE PHRASE "OH, GO FUCK YOURSELF"
She never got to
"Fuck Herself". The line was *too*
Long…way, WAY *too* long.

Whoever said, "The
Truth is ALWAYS best", had *not*
Thought the whole thing through.

Tragedy can be
Not getting what we want, OR…
Can be…*getting it.*

Walls can't "jail" our dreams,
But…day by day they can fade
Away and be lost.

Don't look *too closely*
At your life. Where it IS now…
Perhaps…NOT "the Plan".

"Chores"… *powerful* things.
They keep us from *"pondering"*—
A *deadly* quagmire….

We wonder: Is It
Destiny? Or do we float
On a changing breeze?

Forrest Gump—Ponder
The perfect *wisdom* of a
Fool, and be *amazed!*

What lies behind a
Smile can be Good or Evil.
It's *oft* hard to tell.

Silver-tongued Devils—
Ever a plague upon the
Earth, and on Mankind.

Be *careful* of a
Thing that's *just* what you *want* it
To be…MOST *careful!*

I *avoid* folks of
No responsibility.
My friend seeks them out…

MY CHILDREN…*know* that
I never…ONCE…stopped loving
You…. Truth of *all* truths.

Dogs…never have to
FORGIVE, because they never
BLAME…. They only *LOVE*….

Lovin' him may be
Easy. Livin' with him may
Be…well…*not so much.*

"I can't be *bothered*
With you, but I *LOVE* you." *How*
Does *that REALLY* work???

YOU KNOW THE BALLGAME'S OVER WHEN…
No call…. No text…. No
Breath of sound to testify
He loves you. NOT good!

Is he a "Bearing
Beam" or "Frosting on the Cake"?
Who *cares,* anymore?

EXPECTATION is
The "Mother" of RESENTMENT….
ACCEPT…or *move on….*

Beware "The Midnight
Oil", lest it be YOU who are
Most covered in it.

HE said…. SHE said… And
THEY said. Since you can't believe
Anything…who *knows??*

When you've fallen out
Of love…*everything* they *do*
Is *irritating.*

New friends are very
Good to *have,* but OLD friends are
Most *precious* of all.

Embarrassing things
Are *not* so embarrassing
When you're among *friends.*

"Good" grandmothers BAKE
Cookies and cakes. "Bad" grammas
BUY them. I'm the proof.

Mothers give their last
Breaths to protect their children.
Nature *made* it so.

There's no such thing as
"Growing old gracefully". It's
A bitch 'til the end.

Why must we lose *all*
We WERE and KNEW *before* we
Are allowed to die?

Age and ill-health—the
LEVELERS of beauty, strength
And *all* that *we* were!

Every breath *breathed* leaves
One less breath to take. *Holding*
Your breath won't change things.

"Whistle me up a
Memory...?" No WAY! Can't whist-
Le!!!! Can't *remember!!!!*

My mom wrote notes to
Remember things, but then she
Forgot where they *were.*

EVIDENCE OF THE EXISTENCE OF OUR FIRST and SECOND
CHILDHOODS

"Aiden's chatting in
My ear." "Anything of note?"
"'Course not, Mom…." "He's FOUR!"

"Mom's chatting in my
Ear." "Anything of note?" "'Course
Not…." "She's NINETY-FOUR!"

Thought For The Day: If
Wishes were horses, you'd need
A WHOLE LOT OF HAY!

Racing deals in *flesh*
And *blood*. Horsemen deal in *love*.
What waits at the *wire???*

Horses can't survive
A broken bone. THAT is *why*
They die…. They *are* loved!!!!

If horsemen COULD save
Their horses, they WOULD save them.
NATURE makes the rules.

I have *dreamed* I'd breed
A "Champion". Now…Death is
Near…. The Dream is *gone*.

INTRODUCTION: Shakespeare's *Hamlet* asked that
Greatest of Questions—To BE or NOT to BE?
But there are *other* questions....

Posers, losers and
Boozers.... Which one would you *choose?*
None of the above....

Question: Is it more
Dangerous to HAVE a brain,
Or...NOT to have one?

To wake up next to
Someone you *love,* or NOT to....
THAT is the question.

ARE there as many
"Truths" as pairs of eyes...*looking,*
And brains...*processing?*

How can people who
Are at least fifty percent
WHITE call themselves BLACK?

So *many* "Black Lives
Matter" folks have enough WHITE
Blood to make them WHITE....

"Black Lives Matter" say
"What once *was*...still IS". Then they
Use that *lie* to KILL.

In HISTORY, the
STRONG *overpower* the weak.
"Nature" so *decrees*.

In AMERICA,
The STRONG...*now*...*protect* the weak.
"WOKE" need to AWAKE!

Teaching "Critical
Race" is like teaching *pure HATE*
And *DIVISIVENESS*.

Since Biden became
President, I've understood
PUPPET government.

A wooded-headed
Puppet, tangled in the strings.
A Nation…DESTROYED.

Biden and Cronies
Have *undone* a country forged
By *GREAT thought* and *men*.

Who can make the WORLD
Laugh? Our *Clueless* President
And his *co-felons*.

What *strange* bedfellows!
Our *beloved* Country and
COMMUNIST Regimes….

A weak President,
And the power-seeking "Dems"
Have *taken us DOWN*.

America is
Destroying Itself, as It
Tries to save the World.

Cubans *beg* to be
FREE! We tell them, "Don't come". We'll
Turn you *away!* WHY?

The *rest* of the World…
ILLEGALLY…sneaks *in*. We
WELCOME! We PAY! WHY?

South of the Border….
The plight *North* of the Border….
None left to STOP it !!!!

The Bidens have used
Their connections for *themselves,*
ALONE…through these years.

The Keystone Pipeline???
Who NEEDS it?? We'll just hitch our
Wagons to a STAR!!

"Global *Warming*"—a
FACT OF LIFE on Earth for these
Past *four trillion years*….

Oh *Afghanistan!*
Biden has *forsaken* You….
America *weeps*….

He *so* OFFENDED
People's *pride*, they could not *see*
His WORTH…. Donald Trump.

GOD SAID, "IT IS HARDER FOR A CAMEL TO PASS THROUGH THE EYE OF A NEEDLE THAN FOR A RICH MAN TO ENTER THE KINGDOM OF HEAVEN".

Eye of a Needle—
Kingdom of Heaven—Both are
Hard to *navigate.*

Well…I *guess*…to all
You *rich* Evangelists…I
Will see you in HELL!

I KNOW that Vengeance
Belongs *only* to the Lord…
Because He *said* so!

How can a LOVING
God say, "Vengeance is MINE" *and
STILL remain GODLY?*

God took himself "Off
The Hook" when he gave unto
Man "Free Will". *Good Move!*

God made Man with NO
Knowledge of EVIL, then *left*
Him ALONE with It!

God saw *Evil* in
Men, and sent "The Great Flood". Babes,
Still in the womb…DIED.

Soooo….

Why is a dove with
An olive-branch the symbol
Of *love*, not *murder?!?*

Whoever said, "The
MEEK shall inherit The Earth
Did not have a *CLUE*.